Love is POWER or Something Like that

A. Igoni Barrett

Chatto & Windus

LONDON

Published by Chatto & Windus 2013

First published in the United States of America by Graywolf Press in 2013

2 4 6 8 10 9 7 5 3 1

Copyright © A. Igoni Barrett 2013

A. Igoni Barrett has asserted his right under the Copyright, Designs
and Patents Act 1988 to be identified as the author of this work

First published in Great Britain in 2013 by
Chatto & Windus

Random House, 20 Vauxhall Bridge Road,
London SW1V 2SA

www.randomhouse.co.uk

Addresses for companies within The Random House Group Limited can be found at:
www.randomhouse.co.uk/offices.htm

The Random House Group Limited Reg. No. 954009

A CIP catalogue record for this book
is available from the British Library

ISBN 9780701187392

The Random House Group Limited supports the Forest Stewardship Council® (FSC®),
the leading international forest-certification organisation. Our books carrying the FSC
label are printed on FSC®-certified paper. FSC is the only forest-certification scheme
supported by the leading environmental organisations, including Greenpeace. Our paper
procurement policy can be found at:
www.randomhouse.co.uk/environment

Printed and bound by CPI Group (UK) Ltd, Croydon, CR0 4YY

LOVE IS POWER, OR SOMETHING LIKE THAT

From Caves of Rotten Teeth

For those twin, evergreen pillars of the Oruwari family,
Ineba and Eretoru, and in memory of I. J. Oruwari

And it may be that love sometimes occurs without pain or misery.

—Annie Proulx, *The Shipping News*

Contents

Love Is Power, or Something Like That

The Worst Thing That Happened

For the fourth time in almost as many years, Ma Bille had to go in for eye surgery, this time to have her cataracts removed. She was not afraid: at sixty-eight years of age she had been in and out of the operating room so many times that the antiseptic reek of hospital walls was as familiar to her as the smell of baby poop. The thing that worried her, that made her wake up this morning with her heart hammering in her ears, was the suspicion that she was all alone in a world that had seen the best years of her life.

While she waited for sensation to return to her legs, she ran her mind over the tasks for the day. Her domestic routine, established after her husband's death and perfected in the years since the last of her five children had left the house, was the cogwheel of her existence, the real reason to live. After the last operation she had shuffled around the house for five days with a blindfold of surgical gauze over her eyes, condemned to do nothing but eat, bathe, sit on the toilet bowl, and listen to the sounds of the street outside her window. She had emerged from that invalid's limbo with a renewed zest for workaday duties, but since she noticed the fog creeping in again from the edges of her vision, she had begun to wonder if she was fighting fate.

At first, glaucoma—two failed operations, and one success. Now, cataracts, which, the doctors said, was a complication they had expected. Next time, God knows what else. She was tired of the hospital visits, of the countless eye tests, of the segments of her life that were stolen by anaesthetics. But, especially, she was fed up with the troop of jeans-wearing surgeons who attended to her, who reassured her of complete recovery in happy-go-lucky tones, who declined to describe her ailment in comprehensible language and dismissed as inconsequential her complaints of blistering headaches, of the nausea that was triggered by the flash of bright lights, of the pain that seared her eyeballs night and day. After three operations, all that remained of the worst symptoms were the memories of how she had suffered. Now, quietly, without the theatrics of physical discomfort, her eyesight was fading.

She could feel herself slipping back into sleep, so she pulled aside the duvet and looked down at her legs. The sight of her stumpy, varicose, bunion-knuckled legs never failed to shock her, always seemed to mock her, to impose on her—at the start of each new day—an intimate image of decay. Mr. Bille used to say she had the finest legs in all of Ijoland, and sometimes, God forgive her, she thought it a good thing that he died before he could see what arthritis had done to her legs. The worst thing to happen to you, she said to herself, then dragged her legs to the side of the bed—huffing from the effort and wincing from the shocks of pain that shot through her knees—and edged them over.

When she opened her bedroom door Cardinal Rex loped over to meet her with his tail raised. He rubbed his sides against her ankles, purring and flicking his tail; then he padded after her as she went about her housecleaning, shining his yellow-fever eyes at the back of her head and resting on his haunches to lick his charcoal fur whenever she stopped too long at a spot. After she wedged open the kitchen door and swallowed her morning dose of celecoxib tablets and cod-liver oil capsules washed down with two bottles of lukewarm spring water, she scraped the leftovers of last night's cooking into his green plastic plate. She sat on a shortlegged stool in the center of the courtyard and with a chewing stick cleaned her strong, yellowed teeth. While the morning air washed over her naked, collapsed breasts as she waited for the water on the stove to heat up for her breakfast and bath, Cardinal Rex ate at her feet.

She finished her meal of maize porridge, moinmoin, and Lipton tea, waited for the food to settle in her gut, then rose from the stool and carried her plates to the kitchen sink. Over the sound of running water she heard Cardinal Rex scramble up the fence of the house onto the roof to sun himself. She had lived in this house for thirty-two years, ever since Mr. Bille left her, and for many of those years she had cohabited with cats, yet she still wondered how come every one of the eight cats she had owned at different times always took the same path onto the roof. Her husband had hated cats—they were arrogant and disloyal, unlike dogs, he used to say. There was a time, when he was still alive, that she, too, favored dogs; but now the sight of their eager bodies, the sound of their yaps and bays and yelps and growls, gave her palpitations.

The first Cardinal Rex had been a white female cat. But after seeing the ease with which her coat got smudged, after suffering through the nighttime caterwauls of wooing males, and after what had to happen happened and she woke up one morning to find a litter of four blind kittens that their mother abandoned because she moved them from the rug in the parlor into a cardboard box lined with old handtowels, Ma Bille learned her lesson. When the animosity that bloomed between cat and owner drove the first Cardinal Rex into exile, Ma Bille replaced her with a black male cat. Until his death from stoning at the hands of some neighborhood children who mistook him for a witch's cat, Cardinal Rex the second lived a happy, simple life. It was from his time that she established her routine of feeding her cats twice a day. It was with him that she fell into the habit of talking to her cats, of threatening to withhold their meals when their conduct called for rebuke, of rewarding them with scraps of dried crawfish when they were good.

Her plate washing done, Ma Bille took up the pot of hot water, shuffled to the bathroom, shouldered open the heavy-timbered door, and went in. The bathroom was small, low-ceilinged, and stank of mildew. A colony of chitinous creatures thrived in the wet earth underneath the metal bathtub. She glanced around out of habit to see if any cockroaches had ignored the daylight signal to return to their hiding places, but in the dim lighting, her eyesight failed her.

With her towel around her waist and her bare feet smearing the floor, Ma Bille emerged from the bathroom. The sun was blazing, the ground was awash with light, her eyes were suffused with the brilliance of everyday colors, and as she crossed the courtyard she stepped on something squishy. She halted in surprise, stooped to see better, released her breath in anger, then picked up the half-eaten rat by the scabby tail and tossed it over the fence. Raising her voice so that Cardinal Rex, wherever he was, would hear her, she said:

"No supper for you today, bad pussy!"

On ordinary days, after she took her bath she would slip into one of her old, wash-faded boubous and then walk to God's Time Is Best Supermarket on the street corner to buy a chilled bottle of Harp. She would return home with the beer, go into the kitchen to fetch her beer mug, then carry mug and bottle on a tray to the parlor and place the tray in the chair that stood before the window facing the street. That was where she sat, on the armrest of the chair, sipping her beer, gazing out on the tide of life through the age-browned, flower-patterned lace drapes, until lunchtime.

But today was not an ordinary day. Ma Bille had somewhere to go.

She entered her fluorescent-lit room, stripped off the towel, and tossed it on the bed. She walked to her jumbled dresser and stared in the tall mirror, searching for soapsuds between her legs and mucus in the corners of her eyes. She rubbed palm kernel oil into her halo of thinning hair, cocoa-buttered her skin, drew on her going-out girdle and a white underwired brassiere. She chose her clothes with painstaking care, as she flitted from trunk to mirror and back again. She settled for a yellow brocade blouse and a George wrapper, and once dressed, powdered her face, applied mascara, glossed over the cracks in her lips with brown lipstick, and clasped on a coral-bead necklace and a matching bracelet. She wrapped some money in the knot of her wrapper, stepped into her rubber-soled Bata slippers, then walked to the front door and went out to buy her beer.

She was perched on the armrest, beer mug in hand, when the door of the house across the street crashed open. The house was fenced, but Ma Bille could see the front door through the grilled gate. She pressed her forehead against the window bars and watched as a figure emerged and sat down on the doorstep. She couldn't make out the face—there was once a time when she could see all the way into the courtyard of that house—but she knew for certain it was Perpetua.

In all the years that they had stared into each other's houses and watched one another grow old, Ma Bille and Perpetua had never called each other by name, never held a conversation, never greeted. Perpetua was a widow with only one child whom everybody knew was a drunk who hated her mother. To the scandal of her daughter's condition was added other strangenesses: Perpetua never came out at night; she was the first person on the street to wall up her frontage and the only one who put razor wire in her fence, even though she was poor; she was the widow of one of the first foreign-educated men in Poteko, a man who had streets and government buildings in the city named after him, yet she was poor. Ma Bille had warned her children time and again—when they still lived with her—to avoid "that woman's house," and only her youngest, Nimi, disobeyed: he used to cross the street to sit and chat with Perpetua. Despite that provocation over the years the two women had not found an excuse to quarrel, but Ma Bille blamed Perpetua for the death of Cardinal Rex the second, because it was in front of her house that she had found his broken body.

Ma Bille turned away from the window, muttering with a vehemence that watered her eyes. She lifted her mug, tossed down the warm, bitter remains of her beer, and rose from her seat, carried the mug, empty bottle, and tray into the kitchen, then locked the kitchen door, her bedroom door, and the front door behind her. From her doorstep she scanned the sun-washed street. A FanYogo carton lay on the road, and strawberry yogurt had leaked out and pooled on her paved frontage, a lurid pink surface dive-bombed by flies. Ma Bille walked to the road's edge, looked left, right, left again, and then hurried across. As she approached the other side she heard the murmur of Perpetua's voice, and glanced in through her gate. Perpetua was chatting with a bread hawker, a young mother with a sleeping baby strapped to her back, who knelt beside her wooden tray piled high with oven-fresh bread. She was spreading mayonnaise on a split loaf with slow sweeps of her knife. Ma Bille stared. There was something different about Perpetua—she was wearing a new blouse, a striking shade of blue, like the sky on a bright day, today; and, also, she seemed to have lost weight, she looked younger. Then Ma Bille got it: she had shaved off her hair. At that instant Perpetua looked up and fell silent. The bread hawker turned around. "*E kaaro,* Ma," she greeted, but Ma Bille walked off without answering, her footsteps quickening as Perpetua snickered.

&

It was close to Christmas, there were carnivals and street parties happening everywhere in the city, the roads were jammed with traffic, so the bus ride to her daughter's house, which usually took twenty-five minutes, lasted more than an hour, and cost double the normal fare. When she protested the amount, the bus conductor called her an old soldier and barked at her to get off the bus and use her legs. He was shouted down by the other passengers, several of whom, all men, in response to his taunts, threatened to teach him a lesson they promised he would never forget.

The fourteen-seater Volkswagen bus was packed full. Ma Bille had taken the last spot, the seat beside the open door. The bus conductor leaned over her the entire ride, his shoulders jammed in the doorframe, his hip pressed against her side, his smell of old sweat and unwashed underwear blowing in her face. By the time her stop arrived her legs were shaking. "My lastborn is older than you, you stupid boy!" she hissed at the conductor as she disembarked, but the cornrowed, cashew-juice-tattooed teenager winked at her and whirled round to chase after the moving bus with long, easy strides. She shook her head after him, and then looked around for a respectable stranger to lead her across the busy motorway.

Her last child was thirty-seven years old. He had lived with her until nine years ago, when he traveled to China—via Libya, then Qatar, then Malaysia—in search of a better life. He was married now, to a Filipino woman he had met in a textile plant in Zhengzhou, and they had two children, a four-year-old girl whom they had named Corazon after his wife's mother, and a one-year-old boy who was called Ramón after his wife's father. He had sent his mother their photographs with the last parcel of canned pork and imitation-leather handbags that arrived from him with climatic regularity. The letter that accompanied the parcel informed her he was doing well, that he no longer worked in factories but now tutored Chinese professionals in the English language, and that he might come to visit next year with his family. In her reply she had urged him to come quickly because the eye trouble had recurred, and she wanted to see her grandchildren before she went blind.

Nimi wasn't the only one of her children who had made his home in a foreign land. Her first child, Ineba, lived in the UK, and had been resident there since she left Nigeria with her diplomat husband in 1982. She never sent money, gifts, or letters, and the last time Ma Bille spoke with her—four months ago, on her daughter Alaba's phone—she had scolded her mother for her backwardness in refusing to get herself a mobile phone. Ineba had three children whom their grandmother had never met, and whenever Ma Bille expressed the hope that this oversight would be corrected, Ineba brushed aside her request with a litany of complaints about Nigeria. But Ma Bille expected to meet her first grandchild soon. He was a journalist and wrote for the *Shetland Times,* one of his articles had won a prize that his mother never tired of talking about, and she had told Ma Bille that he planned to visit Nigeria in the coming year to carry out research for the book he was writing about the immigrant experience.

Of all Ma Bille's children, Otonye, her first son, was the first to leave home. He was granted a college athletics scholarship to the US when he was nineteen. She had felt he was too young to travel so far from home, and if he hadn't insisted and threatened to run away, she would not have let him go. She gave him her farewell blessing only after he had promised to steer clear of civil rights marches, to abstain from drugs and alcohol, and, most important of all, to avoid relationships with crazy women, which all white women were. She didn't know if he had kept his word, because the last time anyone in the family had heard from him was twenty-six years ago, when his mother received a Burger King postcard. It was postmarked Champaign, Illinois, and it announced in one short sentence that he had graduated magna cum laude. The script was in a hand that she recognized as her son's, but the name was Tony Billie.

Her fourth child, Ibiso, lived in faraway, sun-ravaged Sokoto, where she was a home economics teacher in a mission school. She was married to Christ, as she curtly informed her mother whenever the issue of her single status cropped up in conversation. Ma Bille did not look forward to her visits, which happened once a year during the Ramadan season, because her born-again daughter dedicated her holidays to saving her mother's soul.

Alaba, her third child, lived in the same city, Poteko, a few miles from her mother's house. She was married to a Trinidadian, the tuba-voiced, hummus-complexioned Amos Stennet, who was a field engineer with Shell. He spent more time on floating rigs in the Bongo oilfields than he did with his family. Whenever he was onshore—as he was now, because of the spate of ransom kidnappings that had caused his company to evacuate all expatriate personnel to the mainland—he made up for the time away by impregnating his wife. Alaba, at forty-two, had seven children, four girls and three boys, the oldest in university, the youngest in kindergarten. Ma Bille doted on them.

∂⊃

The walk from the bus stop to the gate of her daughter's house took seventeen minutes, and Ma Bille was puffing, her forehead dappled with sweat, when the gateman opened to her knock. Alaba lived in GRA—Government Reserved Area, a high-class neighborhood with middle-class antecedents—on a tree-lined street called Springfield Avenue. Her white-stuccoed, villa-style house stood amid a forest of cycads and conifers. The wall around the house was as high as a battleship and it was topped with strings of electrified wire. The winding, gravel-paved driveway that led to the front porch was bordered on both sides by manicured azalea bushes. When Ma Bille stepped onto the porch, the scent from the flowerpots that swung from the ceiling, that hung from the fluted pillars, that lined the floor and balustrade like squat terracotta sentinels with headdresses of vibrant color, made her sneeze.

Ma Bille pressed the doorbell and waited for the housemaid to open for her. A key rattled in the lock, the steel-armored door inched open, and a face appeared. "Alaba!" Ma Bille exclaimed, throwing up her arms.

"Welcome, Ma," Alaba said. She spoke in a low, tired voice, and her face, underneath its bright makeup, was gloomy. She wore a red silk blouse and tight blue jeans. Her nubuck leather waist belt—which was studded with mother-of-pearl, as were her red thong sandals—cinched her blouse over her belly. Her gold-streaked braids were gathered in a ponytail, her fingers and toes were garish with blue nail polish, and around her neck hung a gold necklace dangling a heart-shaped ruby in the cleave of her breasts. As she pushed the door wide and stepped aside for her mother to pass, a blast of eau de cologne wafted through the doorway.

"Where's Tokini? Why are you not at the boutique? What happened?" Ma Bille asked in a rush, and peered into her daughter's face. Alaba did not reply until the door closed.

"It's a long story."

Ma Bille followed her daughter into the high-ceilinged lounge, then sat down in the white leather armchair closest to the French window and jiggled her knees while Alaba headed to the kitchen to fetch some drinking water. As Ma Bille drank, she kept her eyes on Alaba's face, but her gaze clouded over when the cold water stuck in her throat. She choked and spluttered, and beat her chest with her hand. She took a deep breath, ducked her head, and dabbed her eyes with the edge of her wrapper, then straightened and set down the glass.

"Tell me before I die of fear. What has happened?"

With an impassive voice, Alaba said that the housemaid had been dismissed.

"Why?" Ma Bille asked.

"I found out she was pregnant."

"What!"

"I've suspected it for some time, she's been acting funny. But when she was cleaning fish two nights ago she threw up in the kitchen, so I confronted her."

"But how, who . . . *no!*"

"Yes, Ma, it was him."

"Ah! Amos has killed me! Where is he? Let me talk to him!"

"I kicked him out with Tokini. He must fix that problem before he sets foot in this house again. When a man can't keep it in his pants, this is the disgrace."

"But, Alaba, the kidnappers . . ."

"Serves him right if they get him," Alaba said. "Good riddance to bad rubbish."

"Don't say that. Don't say something you'll regret later. What he did was wrong, but he's still your husband. Call him. Let him come back. Let's look for a way to solve this."

Alaba's eyes glistened, her nostrils flared, her lips curled in a snarl, she gripped her knees and leaned forward. "No, no, no, Ma, hundred times no! After seven children, what more does that man want from me? I've not even told you—I'm pregnant again. The few months he's spent at home, he's impregnated me and the house girl together! So all the time he's away, what has he been doing? How many of his bastards are running around the streets?"

Ma Bille shifted her feet and rubbed her palms together. After a long pause, she said: "Please, my daughter, treat this with wisdom. You know what I always say: the worst thing to happen to you—"

Alaba cut her off. "Yes, Ma. I know what you always say."

They relapsed into silence. The house was alive with electronic noises: the whirr and screak of the ceiling fan, the hum of the refrigerator, the sporadic clicking of the stabilizer; but it was the faraway, persistent woofing of a dog that broke into Ma Bille's thoughts. She cocked her head, listening to the sound. Her blunt-nailed, wizened hands twitched in her lap.

"You're thinking about them, aren't you?"

Ma Bille looked up to find her daughter staring at her; the expression on Alaba's face was hidden by the fog that followed Ma Bille's gaze like a wilful shadow.

"Yes," Ma Bille replied.

"They were just dogs." Alaba leaned forward, so her face jumped into focus. "It was a long time ago, you should forget it. There are more important things to worry about."

"Alaba," Ma Bille said, holding her daughter's gaze, "one day you will see that the only important things in this life are your memories. So leave me with my own."

"All right," Alaba said. She folded her arms across her belly and pursed her lips, then changed the subject. "So why did you come? You know I'm at the boutique around this time."

"I wanted to see Amos. I was planning to wait around till you returned."

"I hope no problem?"

"My operation is tomorrow."

"Hah, I forgot. This eye problem even, it's getting too much. This is the third time, isn't it? I hope you're not afraid?"

"No—fourth time," Ma Bille said. "I'm not afraid. But I need someone to follow me to the hospital. I was hoping it would be Amos, but with this thing he has done, it will have to be you."

The barking had ceased. From the treetops outside, birds twittered.

Ma Bille spoke. "All other times I've gone alone, so you know I wouldn't ask if it wasn't important. The nurses these days are not very nice, and they're overworked anyway. It's not that I can't go by myself, but they'll bandage my eyes, so I won't see. The last time after the operation I woke up at night with a running stomach, and I stayed in that hospital bed calling for more than an hour, yet nobody came. I had to crawl out of the ward on my knees, because I kept banging my legs against the beds."

"I'm sorry, Ma. I didn't know it was like that."

"It's okay," Ma Bille said. "Old age has its lessons too."

"But it's not okay!" Alaba burst out. Ma Bille stared at her in surprise, and kept on staring as Alaba shot out of the chair and paced the room, her braids swinging, her hands chopping the air, the slate-flat heels of her thong sandals slapping the terrazzo. "I mean, what will people say when they hear that my mother crawled on the hospital floor, a public hospital for that matter? That is the height of suffering—and yet you have children who can afford to send you abroad for treatment! But where is Otonye, ehn, where is that one? He just disappeared in America like a person who has no background. And see Ineba, with her *fri-fri* talk, like it is British accent we will eat. As for Nimi, he's the youngest, he should be here taking care of you instead of sending all those fake Chinese bags that anybody can buy in bend-down market!"

"Alaba . . ."

"No, Ma, I have to tell you my mind. It's not fair! All of them are abroad enjoying their lives, but look at me, look at my life, look at what Amos has done to me. I can't be the only one doing everything. Taking care of my children, taking care of my husband, taking care of my mother, going to my boutique every day because all those girls I hired are thieves! I have seven children, plus another one coming, and now Amos has gone to give my house girl belleh! Nobody can take me for granted o! I'm not a donkey that will be carrying everybody's—"

Ma Bille raised her hand. "Sit down, Alaba. You're giving me a headache."

Alaba strode to the seat opposite Ma Bille and dropped into it. She crossed her leg, clutched the arms of the chair like it was hurtling through the air, and stared into space, scowling.

"Everybody has their own life to live," Ma Bille said quietly. "I don't expect anybody to come and take care of me. I don't ask any of you to feed me. All I'm asking is that you follow me to the hospital for my operation tomorrow."

"But I can't, don't you see?" Alaba said. She stretched her hands, palms open, toward her mother. "I have to be in the house when the driver brings the children from school. I can't leave them alone, I have to cook for them. If Tokini was still around then I would have followed you, no problem, but I can't, not now, not until I get a new house girl."

Ma Bille opened her mouth to speak, but shut it without making a sound. She bowed her head, stared into her lap, struggled to compose her face. One word rose above the hubbub in her head—*abandonment*. Her husband, her youth, her health, her sight even: all had abandoned her. Her children, too, had abandoned her. All the years she had given, the sacrifices, the worrying, the love—everything she gave, she gave for nothing.

"No, not for nothing," she murmured. "I gave because I wanted to."

Alaba glanced at her. "What did you say, Ma? I didn't catch that."

Ma Bille raised her eyes, stared at her daughter's face, searching its contours for traces of the child she had breastfed, whose nose she had sucked mucus from, whose mouth had opened wide to gulp food from her fingers. Memories shuffled through her head, blinding her with images. When that face was seven years old, the child had tripped over a broom and gashed her forehead against the dining table, right there, where that scar glistened beneath the face powder. At seventeen, she had come first in her class, and as a treat Ma Bille took her to the Chinese restaurant that used to be on the third floor of Chanrai House. When she was in her final year in university—she was twenty-three then—Ma Bille sold her finest pieces of gold jewelry, presents from her late husband, to the black-market merchants on Adaka Boro Street, to pay Alaba's fees. That night, when Alaba came home from the hostel to collect the money, she hugged Ma Bille and whispered against her cheek, "I love you, Ma."

I love you too, Alaba, Ma Bille thought, gazing at her daughter's averted face. All the support she had given, and she still gave, accompanying her daughter to the hospital whenever she went into labor, bathing her grandchildren when they were babies, feeding them, rocking them to sleep, passing on to her daughter the tricks of child caring—everything she gave, she gave because she wanted to.

Ma Bille said her daughter's name.

"Yes?" Alaba answered in a sullen tone, and sneaked a look at her mother.

"That belt you're wearing, it's too tight. Go and remove it. It's not good for the baby."

℘

The children were happy to see their grandmother. Every time Ma Bille responded to the greedy questions they shot at her—all six of them who had tumbled into the house in a storm of dust and noise—she said their names: Wariso, Sekibo, Owanari, Nimi (whom everyone except her called Small Nimi), Ibinabo, and Dein. The oldest of Alaba's children, Enefaa, who was studying for a law degree at the University of Jos, was Ma Bille's namesake. Amos had insisted that his children be given native names, and Ma Bille, whenever she had the chance, instructed her son-in-law on the pronunciations, explained the meanings, described the idiomatic treasures of his children's names.

It was evening when Ma Bille stood up to leave. The driver had closed for the day and Alaba was too busy with the children to drive her mother home, but it didn't matter, because Ma Bille said she wanted to walk to the bus stop. The exercise was good for her legs, she told her daughter.

Six-year-old Ibinabo escorted her from the house, singing in a breathless voice and skipping circles around her grandmother. Her smooth legs flashed; her bare feet scattered gravel on the path. The gateman emerged from his cubicle, pulled open the gate, and Ibinabo crooned her good-bye, then whirled round and raced up the driveway toward the house. Ma Bille passed through the gateway and headed down the road she had come, her footsteps dragging. The road ahead was empty, darkened by twilight, bleak. As Ma Bille approached the fence of the next compound she heard a strange noise behind her, turned around to look, and froze.

A dog stood before her, near enough that she could smell its earthy odor. It was a big one, an outsized beast: its thick legs were splayed under the weight of its trunk. Its short-haired coat was brindled, brown and black, and a ruff of spiky fur grew over its shoulder and down the curve of its spine. A studded collar was fastened around its neck, and the leather leash snaked between its legs. It grinned at Ma Bille, its tongue lolling, its tail stump twitching.

"Don't worry—don't be afraid." The speaker, a blond, teenaged girl, approached Ma Bille at a saunter. She was panting. "Here, Granbull, here, boy—woohoo!" she said to the dog, and stooped to pick up the leash. "Let's leave the nice lady alone."

When she tugged the leash, the dog opened its mouth and let out a boom. Then another, and another, each bark deeper, more ferocious. It resisted the girl's desperate pulling without taking its heavy-lidded eyes off Ma Bille. Its red, serrated lips flapped and quivered.

"Behave, Granbull!" the girl commanded. She threw Ma Bille a close-lipped smile. "He's never acted this way before. Maybe he knows you?"

"No, it's not that," Ma Bille said. "I have the blood of five dogs on my hands."

The dog was still barking, its snout flecked with foam, and the girl was staring, her eyes round with shock, when Ma Bille turned and walked away.

She remembered their names, all five of them. "One for you to name and look after," her husband had said to each of the children every time he brought home a round-bellied Alsatian puppy. It was Ineba who started the trend in beverages. She was gifted the first dog, and she named it Whiskey after her father's favorite drink. Three months later, when Otonye got his dog, he told his sister, "Now Whiskey has her Brandy." Alaba called hers Sherry, because, she said, the name sounded aristocratic. Ibiso, even then, had faith only in what she knew, so she called her dog Cocoa. Nimi chose Coffee, because Beer or Tea or Coke did not sound to him like names even a dog would bear.

The dogs, all five of them, died on the same day thirty-six years ago, on a hot July afternoon. Because the sun was out and it was a public holiday, Ma Bille had instructed the children to wash the animals. After the bath, the dogs were tethered to the verandah railing so that they would not roll in the yard and soil their wet coats. Ma Bille was in the parlor darning school uniforms and listening to Boma Erekosima on FM radio when Nimi entered in tears and told her Coffee was suffering. She went outside to see for herself what the matter was. In the struggle to free themselves the dogs had entangled their chains, and they were bunched together in one corner of the verandah, where the floor was puddled with dog-hair-colored water and scattered with dogshit. The dogs whined and yowled, strained against their chains, looked dejected. They were plagued by a buzzing swarm of flies. Ma Bille directed the children to unravel the chains and clean up the mess, but even after the floor was washed with Izal disinfectant, the flies remained. The dogs shook themselves fiercely, and snapped at the air, and ducked their heads, but the flies circled and swooped, tormenting them. In a final exasperated effort Ma Bille fetched the can of Baygon insecticide from her bedroom and sprayed the floor, the walls, the flies, the dogs. The flies dropped out of the air, the dogs lay down in relief, Nimi wiped his tears, and Ma Bille went back inside to catch her radio program. Ten minutes later the dogs began to howl, and they did not cease this racket until they were stretched out in all corners of the yard, their coats sodden with diarrhea and blood and vomit, their jaws locked in the snarl of death.

It was the worst time of her life: the guilt, the grief, the pileup of disasters. Two days later, two days after she killed the dogs, Mr. Bille suffered the final heart attack. There had been no time for forgiveness, no time to coax him out of the silence that followed his explosion of rage at the news of the dogs' deaths. One morning he rose and left for work without replying to her greeting or eating her food, and by evening he was dead.

But for her children, she would not have survived. The catastrophe that collapsed her world exposed her children's toughness. They stood by her in her darkest hour, frightened out of their mourning by the intensity of hers, pleading, consoling, urging restraint as she rolled around in bed and beat her fists, as she retched when the tears would no longer seep from her stinging eyes, as she wallowed in guilt and snot, embraced her grief along with her pillows, and turned her back on life, hope, self-control. Her children fought her with common sense and coerced her with love. They reminded her of the times the doctors had warned their father to give up smoking and alcohol and to adjust his eating habits; they told her, *the dogs' deaths don't matter, the dogs' deaths don't matter, the dogs' deaths don't matter,* until, one day, the dogs' deaths didn't matter. The worst thing that happened to her revealed the best thing she had.

ℬ

When Ma Bille turned into her street, the security lamps on the front walls of the queued houses were glinting dully in the dusk. She stopped opposite her house, looked left, right, left again, then placed her foot on the road and looked right, just in time to glimpse a shape streaking across her frontage. Cardinal Rex, wherever he'd been, had seen her, she thought.

"That was a rat. They're getting bigger and bigger these days."

Ma Bille spun around, wincing as her joints creaked. But when her eyes—squinting, straining in the gathering darkness—confirmed what her ears had heard, she forgot about her pain. It *was* Perpetua.

Her gate hung open, which, given the lateness, was unusual; and, even stranger, Perpetua was still sitting in the darkened doorway of her house, as if she hadn't moved since morning. Ma Bille sniffed loudly to mask her amazement, and slowly, deliberately, turned away. She hurried across the road, unlocked her front door, then stood on her doorstep, one leg in and one leg out, stared into the darkness, the loneliness of her house. She pulled the door shut and walked back across the road. She entered Perpetua's gate, halted in front of her, and said, "How come it's today you're talking to me, after all these years?"

Perpetua raised her hand to slap away a cloud of mosquitoes. "I don't beg anybody for friendship," she said, her voice assured, careful with pronunciation.

There seemed nothing left to say, and Ma Bille's legs ached.

"I should go," Ma Bille said.

"I know—time to feed your cat."

"Yes."

Ma Bille did not move. She wondered if she should ask. It wasn't her business, but Perpetua had reached out, broken the silence. For a reason.

In a cautious tone, Ma Bille asked, "Is there a problem?"

"No," Perpetua said.

"Are you sure? I've never seen you outside this late before."

"Yes, I'm sure," Perpetua said. "It's just that my legs have refused to work."

"Ah." Ma Bille clicked her teeth together. "Sorry, I know the feeling. My legs do the same thing every morning." She paused. "Should I help you inside?"

"I'll be grateful," Perpetua said.

Ma Bille started forward, and Perpetua leaned aside to let her pass through the doorway, then raised her arms so that Ma Bille could grasp her by the armpits. Ma Bille pulled up the smaller woman, clasped her to her chest, and then dragged her into the house with backward steps. After a drawn-out, exhausting effort, Ma Bille eased Perpetua into a chair in the parlor, and then dropped into the adjoining seat, blowing hard and dabbing her face with the edge of her wrapper, her free hand rubbing her shaking knee.

When her heart rate calmed, Ma Bille pushed herself to her feet. Perpetua's house was the same floor plan as hers, and in the dark, she could have been at home. She walked to the window and drew the curtains closed, then felt along the wall for the light switch and snapped it on. Perpetua was sprawled in the armchair, her arms dangling over the sides and her legs stretched out before her. Her ankles were swollen to the size of her calves.

"How are your legs?" Ma Bille asked.

"Still dead." Perpetua passed a hand over her short dapple-gray hair. "It's my arthritis. I'll have to find a way to get to the hospital tomorrow."

"Which one?"

"College Hospital."

Ma Bille walked to the open door and gazed out for long seconds, then turned back into the room. "I'm going to College Hospital tomorrow for my eye operation," she said. "In the morning, around ten . . ." In the warm light, she caught the gleam of Perpetua's teeth. She smiled back. "The blind leading the lame, no?"

At Ma Bille's words, Perpetua looked down at her legs, the set of her head as expressive as a sigh.

"Don't worry, it will be okay, these things happen for a reason," Ma Bille said. "As I always say: the worst thing to happen to you is for the best—"

"*Sometimes,*" the two old women said together, and stared at each other in surprise, then burst out laughing, their voices ringing through the house and across the street.

Dream Chaser

This morning, same as other mornings that he skipped school, fifteen-year-old Samu'ila pushed open the glass swing door and stepped into the chilled air of the cybercafe. It was a long room, a converted warehouse, and there was no ventilation other than the doorway, which was always shut. High on the wall at each end of the room two antiquated air conditioners wheezed and juddered from the flux of electric current and puffed clouds of frost. Harsh white light poured from the ceiling, and a red plush rug, scuffed to brown down the middle by the tramp of feet, covered the floor. The length of the room was lined on both sides with wooden tables, on which sat computer monitors. Beneath the tables stood CPUs and UPSs, with their red, green, and yellow lights flashing, and on the ground, where the red of the rug was still as bright as the day it left the loom, a tangle of wires slithered in and out of everything.

The walls were pasted with notices that warned off fraudsters, spammers, and hackers. As Samu'ila halted before the attendant's desk he saw a poster on the wall, a new one, which read:

We are pleased to announced to you
That our overnight browsing is now
N250!!!
We promise you that you will surely
Going to have a great night with us,
As you come.
We are here to make a different.
Signed: THE MGT

The attendant was a young, pretty woman. She wore sky-blue jeans, tight from hip to ankle, and a pink halter with a décolletage that made Samu'ila suck in his breath: he could see all the way to the rims of her areolas. Atop her head was perched a stiff wing of acrylic hair extension. Her feet—with their long, curved, Smarties-colored toenails—were propped on the desk, crossed at the ankles. She was reading a glossy paperback, which she held in front of her face like a compact mirror. Samu'ila coughed to draw her attention. She did not raise her eyes from the book. He was used to her ways.

"Which book are you reading today, auntie?" he asked.

"Love's Brazen Fire," she replied. Then, with a sigh, she swung her feet off the desk and slammed down the book. "Why won't you people leave me alone!" she snapped as she glanced up. Her eyes flickered with recognition, and, "You again," she said, her voice flat, resigned. "Don't you go to school at all? How much time do you want today?"

"Four hours." Samu'ila held up his hand with his thumb folded.

The attendant extended the ticket to Samu'ila with one hand and stowed his money in the desk drawer with the other. Then she announced, with the singsong of a catechismal recitation:

"The printer is out of order. If the computer hangs, restart it. If it takes forever to open a page, I am not the server. Please, don't call me for anything."

Used to her ways, Samu'ila said, "I know."

She picked up her book, put up her feet. Samu'ila leaned forward to check the time on her mobile phone, which lay on the desk. It was 8:23 a.m.—he straightened, turned around—and yet the cyber-cafe was almost full. He saw an unoccupied computer at the back of the room. He started toward it, and walked into a blast of cold air; the spot he'd chosen was in the path of the second air conditioner. He ignored the cold, pulled out the chair, sat down, cracked his knuckles, blew out his breath through pursed lips, drew out the keyboard panel, and punched in his ticket password. The computer screen flickered alive. With a wide grin Samu'ila bent forward and tip-tapped his way into the phantasmagorical realm of the World Wide Web.

There was an offline message in his Messenger box.

Where are you? I need to chat with you now! Please!!! Lotsa love . . .

The message was from Ben. Ben: the sexagenarian widower whom he had met three weeks ago in an online dating chat room. Ben: the wealthy American retiree with no children and five dogs. Ben: the lonely old man who would do anything for him. Or so he said.

An instant message box popped up on the screen. It buzzed without sound, one time, two times, three times.

You there?

Samu'ila typed his reply.

Yes luv.

Hi sweetie! Where've you been? I've been waiting forever for you to come online . . .

I'm sooo sori dearie, I had some problems @ home. Missed u lots!

Missed you too! Watch the screen . . . have I got a surprise for you!

Samu'ila waited, his fingers poised over the keyboard. The chat box showed no typing activity, so he placed his hands on his head, interlocked his fingers, and leaned back in the chair. He stifled a yawn as his eyes traveled the room. His attention was drawn to the front: the man sitting at the computer beside the attendant's desk was talking into his mobile phone. The man's voice was loud and un-abashed: bank details, professional credentials, and payment figures spilled from his mouth. His left hand waved in the air as he chattered into the phone clutched in his right; his flailing hand was at odds with the cajoling of his tone. A smile spread over Samu'ila's face as he listened to the thickness of the man's accent, the obviousness of his Americanese; but the smile dissolved when the man tossed the phone on the table and, with a shout of joy, high-fived himself.

Samu'ila returned his gaze to the screen in front of him, his thoughts occupied with drafting a phrase that would convey the right mix of surprise and gratefulness. A webcam request appeared on the screen, and, on reflex, he clicked ACCEPT, only realizing what he'd done when a pair of eyes blinked at him.

"Ah!" he cried out, and jolted back his chair in alarm.

The eyes stared straight at Samu'ila, pupils digital gray, whites gleaming. Then the eyes drew back from the camera and Ben's face swung into focus. The webcam picture was grainy, the movements were delayed and disconnected, and Ben's skin was sea-bottom white in the darkness that framed his face.

Samu'ila raised his hand, pinched his nose, pulled it, and scratched his cheek. The eyes on the screen, so far away and yet so near, made him feel naked, exposed. Then Ben lowered his eyes, ducked his head, and a splash of large red text appeared in the chat box.

Can you see me?

Samu'ila released his breath and glanced around to see if anyone had noticed his discomfort. When he turned back to the computer there was a screed of instant messages. Let the old guy suffer small, he said to himself. He watched the face in the screen, noting the comb-teeth eyebrows, the pocked nose and squeezed nostrils, the discolored bags of skin under bulging eyes. It was only when Ben began to send "pleases" that stretched from end to end of the chat box that Samu'ila relented, and typed his reply.

I can c u.

ᛒꝍ

The first time Samu'ila entered a cybercafe, he was sent by his older brother to deliver a love letter to a girl his brother hadn't the courage to approach himself. Samu'ila was eleven years old. He thought the cybercafe was some sort of game arcade for adults, but he soon discarded that idea, convinced of the seriousness of the proceedings in that room by the examinations-hall intensity that hung over it. Word had reached him about the Internet, cyberspace, the World Wide Web, but he hadn't a clear idea of what it was. He had suffered the usual run of fantastical stories that were the stock-in-trade of schoolboys. He had heard that one could watch any movie and music video on the Internet for free. He had been wowed by the revelation that anybody could play any computer game of their choice with an opponent across the world. He'd had his dreams hijacked by the story of the girl who sent love letters to a boy she didn't know, who, when he opened them, was transported to her bedroom to watch as she lay naked and performed magic tricks with a cucumber. He had been told that any item, from a paper clip to a cruise on an ocean liner, could be purchased on the Internet with a mouse; that there were machines called "search engines" that manufactured answers when questions were fed into them. He did not believe these stories, not until the day he stood behind his brother's love interest and watched with glazed eyes as she proved that everything he had discounted was true.

In the early days, when his compulsion still had the glow of innocence, Samu'ila used his childhood charm to extract from his parents little amounts of money. His excuse was candy, but he saved up every kobo to spend in the nearest cybercafe. When his father complained that he would lose all his teeth to rot, and his mother rolled her eyes and sent him off to his father, Samu'ila, to maintain his habit, began to steal.

The day Samu'ila turned fourteen his father sat him down for a man-to-man talk and asked him what he wanted to become in life. When he said, "A doctor," his father laughed long and hard and then turned serious again and said, "No, not what you think I want you to become, but what *you* want." Succumbing to sincerity, Samu'ila confessed that all he wanted to do was sit in front of a computer and surf the Web. His father was shocked by this evidence of a malingering spirit in his son. To absolve himself of blame, he told the boy:

"Do whatever you want, my son, but make sure you make money doing it."

Samu'ila took his father's advice to heart. He opened his eyes and noticed he was the only one in the cybercafes he frequented who wasn't there to make money. All around him were 419ers and green-card gamblers, credit-card thieves and e-mail hackers, software pirates and cyber impersonators—hope merchants and dream chasers all of them, but rooted in reality by the pursuit of money. He, too, would make money, he decided. As part of his plan, Samu'ila played truant at school, and turning his transport and lunch allowance into seed money, he dedicated his time to expanding his Internet knowledge.

By the time Samu'ila met Ben, he had become as proficient with the mores of cyberspace as a worker ant with its duties. He could register e-mail accounts in French, German, Italian, Spanish, and Portuguese. He could download and upload giga-bytes, convert and compress .abc through .xyz file extensions. He could extract e-mail addresses, generate bogus online per-sonas, and spam whole country populations with the click of a mouse. He owned eleven e-mail accounts, all of them with dif-ferent names and nationalities. When he gatecrashed the dat-ing chat room where he spotted Ben, he was masquerading as a twenty-three-year-old Liberian widow who was stranded in Nigeria without friend, family, or hope. Ben took one look at his profile photo—which he had lifted from the obituary of a drowned actress on the Web site of a Martinique newspaper—and fell in love.

᠄

Ben's head was bent over the keyboard as he typed. His curly gray hair had a hairless patch at the crown.

So . . . what do you think?

Samu'ila's reply was prompt.

About?

He knew what Ben meant, but in the role of a woman he always acted difficult or played the fool. That was a cardinal rule.

About me! Are you surprised? Disappointed?

PLESANTLY SUPRISED!!!

Thanks!

Ur welcum :)

Ben's next question drew a smirk on Samu'ila's face.

When will I get to see your face?

His reply:

U've already sin it.

I don't mean your photo. I mean see you as you are seeing me . . . via webcam.

A smile playing on his lips, Samu'ila bent forward to type.

But I've told u be4 Ben, many cafes around here dont hav webcam & I cant afford de money 2 be browsin in de ones dat hav. Its not so easy 4 me 2 be comin 2 chat wit u everyday, its just dat I luv u & I need 2 talk 2 u but it is gettin very hard 2 find de money.

Samu'ila folded his arms against the air conditioner's draft and waited for Ben's reply.

Why don't you call me? Or give me your number so I can call you?

Bcos I dont hav a fone!!!

You don't have a friend whose cell you can borrow for 5 mins?

Ben watched the camera with an intensity that resembled distrust. Samu'ila noticed that his eyes were so light they seemed myopic, and that his nose was hooked at the tip, like a vulture's beak. The air conditioner's gusts were getting colder. Samu'ila decided to end the chat.

I'm startin 2 tink ur only interested in my body . . . 2day it's my face, 2moro it will be my boobs ur wantin 2 c! Ur soundin like all dose men who've tried 2 take advantage of me, like dose rebels in

*Liberia dat killed my husband . . . & I REALY thot u were different!
U've made me feel bad Ben. Bad and dirty. Like a SLOT!!!*

Ben's exclamation-mark riddled "sorry" popped into the chat box, but Samu'ila forged on:

U want 2 c my face, but what about me? U tink I dont want 2 be wt u rite now in ur room, with my head on ur sholder & ur arms around me, holdin me safe? BUT I CANT!!!

Samu'ila leaned back in his seat, clasped his hands together and thrust them between his knees, stared up at the ceiling, ignoring the words on the screen. Then he bent forward, his hands rose and, after hovering over the keyboard in a butterfly dance, swooped.

U dont appreciate all de sacrifice dat I make 2 be here 4 u EVERYDAY!!! U dont even ask why I'm not @ work. 4 de past 3 wks I've been online wt u every morning & u dont even wonder how I'm survivin? Or even if I hav a job? DO U LUV ME @ ALL!?

Ben's eyes darted and blinked, his face creased in distress, his messages flooded in, but Samu'ila closed the instant message box, signed out of his Messenger account, and logged off his ticket. As the computer screen blanked off, he caught his reflection. He wiped the grin off his face. There was still a lot of work to be done on the mugu, and celebrating beforehand, as everybody knew, was bad luck. But even this thought couldn't dampen the good feeling that fizzed in his belly.

He stood up shivering from his chair, cupped his elbows in his palms, and walked quickly to the computer beside the attendant's desk, which the man with the heavy Igbo accent had finished using. As he settled into the lucky seat, the attendant glanced up from her book, caught his gaze, and hissing with annoyance, yanked up her blouse. Then she returned to chapter twenty-eight of her romantic saga.

As for Samu'ila: he signed in this time as a fifteen-year-old Mozambican girl—a virgin, and looking.

The Shape of a Full Circle

Well, son, I'll tell you:
Life for me ain't been no crystal stair.

—Langston Hughes, *Mother to Son*

· 1 ·

Dimié Abrakasa was fourteen years old. He had small ears, a long neck, and the sensitive, flexible fingers of a pickpocket. His grandmother said his skin was the color of polished camwood. His mother hated his eyes.

· 2 ·

The house that bore the number 197 on Adaka Boro Street was painted a sunny-sky blue. On the wall above the doorway, in drippy black paint, were written the words:

THIS HOUSE IS NOT FOR SALE
BEWARE OF 419

The street door, which was ajar because of a broken latch, opened into a corridor that smelled of kerosene smoke and rat fur. The corridor had nine doors on each side, and led into a courtyard. The courtyard served as a store, a kitchen, and a place of social gathering.

· 3 ·

Dimié Abrakasa entered the corridor. He walked to his apartment, the fifth door on the right, and turned the handle. Despite the gentleness of his touch, the door opened with a squeal. The heat that wafted out had the force of a chemical combustion. Dimié Abrakasa unshouldered his school backpack, then walked in and nudged the door closed with his heel. The TV was on. Méneia and Benaebi were home.

"Welcome, Dimié," his brother and sister greeted in unison.

"Ehn," he answered, and looked at his mother. "Afternoon, Mma."

Daoju Anabraba lay on the bed, on her side, her face turned toward the door. From chest to knee she was wrapped in a red, black, and green wax print cloth. Her skin shone with sweat; the bedsheet—pale green, with white flowers patterned across it—was limp with dirt. An empty Gordon's Gin bottle rested on its side on the floor beside the bed. Dimié Abrakasa waited for her to reply to his greeting, which he knew she wouldn't, so he turned and walked to the corner to remove his school uniform.

A single electric bulb hung from the ceiling and lit the room. There was a window in the wall that faced the door, but the wooden shutters were fastened with nails. The bed was lined against this wall. At the foot of the bed stood a sturdy, antique redwood dresser; on its varnished top sat a gilt-framed photograph. Dimié Abrakasa stripped to his underpants in front of the dresser, then pulled open the bottommost drawer and rummaged in it until he found a pair of jeans and his yellow T-shirt.

Méneia and Benaebi sat cross-legged in front of the TV. The light that streamed from the screen played on their still faces. Méneia was the spitting image of her mother, except that, where Daoju Anabraba had a beauty spot on her right cheek, Méneia, in the same place, sprouted a mole that was the size and appearance of a raisin. She was four years older than Benaebi, who, at eight years old, was shedding his milk teeth. He sucked his thumb.

His sister had tried everything in her power to wean him off this habit—from soaking his hands in bitterleaf sap to coating his fingers with chicken shit—but Benaebi persisted. When he wasn't chewing his fingernails, his thumb was thrust through the gaps in his teeth. Several fingers of his two hands were cicatrized by whitlow, and the skin of his thumbs was as pale and shrivelled as lab specimens floating in a jar of formalin.

Dimié Abrakasa moved away from the dresser, and Méneia turned to face him, but her gaze remained on the screen.

"What are we eating, Dimié?" she asked.

Dimié Abrakasa walked to the head of the bed, rested his shoulders against the wall, and said: "There's still garri in the house, abi?"

"But no soup," Méneia replied.

Benaebi looked up, eyes glistening. "I'm hungry," he said, as he sucked his thumb.

"What will we eat?" Méneia asked again.

Dimié Abrakasa glanced at his mother. Her face was closed, heavy as stone. Tendrils of lank brown hair clung to her cheek and fluttered each time she breathed out. Dimié Abrakasa turned back to Méneia. "Like how much do you think we need to cook enough soup to last till tomorrow?"

"Three hundred," Méneia said, after a quick calculation.

"With fish or meat?"

"Meat."

"Fish is cheaper."

"But we used fish for the last two pots of soup!"

Her older brother made no reply, and Méneia, with a sigh, said, "Okay, fish. Two hundred will be enough. Or what do you think?"

"Yes," Dimié Abrakasa said. "I have—" he turned out his pockets, producing clumps of paper and wisps of lint and some naira notes, "—one hundred and six, seven . . . I have one hundred and seventy naira. What of you?"

"I have only ten naira, Dimié."

"Bring it. And you, Benaebi?"

"I'm hungry," Benaebi mumbled at the TV screen.

Méneia swung her head to look at him. "Benaebi!" she snapped, "remove that hand from your mouth before I slap you! *Boo-boo-boo* baby! Do you have any money?"

"I have fifty naira but I'm not giving you!"

"I've heard. Where is it?"

"I said I'm not—"

"Will you shut up? Where's the money?"

"I gave it to Mma this morning."

All eyes turned to the bed. Méneia broke the silence. "H'm," she sniffed, "that one is gone. What should we do, Dimié?"

"We have one-eighty," Dimié Abrakasa said. He counted the notes, folded them into a wad, and stuck it in his right hip pocket. "Let me see—"

His words were cut off by a sudden, cataclysmal darkness. A power cut.

"Aw, NEPA!" Benaebi exclaimed, slapping his thigh. "Dog shit!"

"Shut up," his sister said, "they'll bring it back soon." Then she added: "By God's grace."

Dimié Abrakasa edged round the sound of their voices. The subterranean dark, the stench of degraded alcohol, the whispering heat, had turned the room unbearable for him. He reached the door, pulled it open, emerged into the corridor. When he turned to shut the door, he met his mother's gaze. She raised herself on one elbow, combed back her tousled hair with her fingers, and said, "Don't even think of coming back to this house without my medicine."

· 4 ·

Dimié Abrakasa stepped into the harsh light of midafternoon. On the horizon, he saw a mass of bruise-dark clouds bearing down on the sun. The air was heavy, there was no wind. Rain was approaching. Dimié Abrakasa considered shortcutting through the back streets, but he remembered the money in his pocket, so headed for the open road.

The 1.3 kilometer Ernest Ikoli Road, started in September 1970 and finished nine months later, was for many years extolled—on account of its wideness and its drainage system, its gardened roundabouts and traffic lights and cat's-eyes lane markers—as the model Nigerian city road, the road of the bright future. Once charcoal-black, the road was now an ash-gray stream that threw off sparks where the metal of embedded bolts and bottle tops caught the sunlight. Potholes strewed the asphalt, and the concrete sidewalks were shot with cracks. The roadside drains were silted over in some places, and trash choked in others. The revving engines and horn blares of commuters, the clang-and-bang of artisans, the roar of a populace world-famous as a loudmouthed lot, beat the air. Theme music of city life.

After he passed Number II Sand Field and crossed the road to avoid an approaching pushcart piled high with yams, Dimié Abrakasa felt the urge to urinate. He stopped, looked around, moved forward a few steps, reached the mouth of the alley he'd spotted, and turned into it. The alley was in shadow. Relief from the sun's glare heightened the pressure on his bladder, and he picked his way across the alley, holding his breath. The alley floor was dotted with shit mounds; the air stank of old urine. The windows of the story buildings that formed the sides of the alley were boarded up, and paint flakes curled off the lichened walls. A group of boys was gathered at the alley end.

Dimié Abrakasa halted, opened his fly, and ignoring the faded letters on the wall in front of him that spelled,

DO NOT UNIRATE OVERHERE ANYMORE

BY ORDER! THE LANDLORD

he splashed the wall. He arched his back and sighed in release, then shifted his foot to avoid the foaming stream. A thrill of excitement entered the boys' voices. As he squeezed out the last drops, the boys raised a cheer—a shriek of agony rent the air. Startled, he jumped, and his fly-zipper snagged his flesh. He yelped with pain, and sucked in his breath. Then, with careful fingers, he freed himself from the grip of the zipper teeth.

Giving in to a curiosity so intense he could smell its cat breath, Dimié Abrakasa approached the boys. They made way; they absorbed him into their ranks. As he'd suspected, it was something subhuman they had ganged up on. He'd expected to see a mangy dog, or a goat lying in a pool of blood, but he found he was staring at the cowering form of a rag-draped madwoman. She was crouched on the ground in the center of the circle formed by the boys. Her knees were drawn up to her chest and her hands covered her ears. The skin of her knees was scabrous; her hands were tree-root grimy. Her hair fell on her shoulders in thick, brownish clumps, and it was sprinkled with the confetti of garbage dumps. She reeked of disease.

Dimié Abrakasa turned his gaze to the boys. He counted heads, but when he got to the twelfth, someone moved to a new position, distracting him, and he was too close to the end to bother starting over. Some boys held sticks in their hands, others clutched bricks, and a few had both. He recognized two boys as schoolmates, but every other person was a stranger.

He looked again at the madwoman. She was growling, the sound buzzed at the rim of her teeth, and she rocked on her heels. Her eyes were bloodshot with fear and yet her expression was calm. Her gaze roamed the circle—she swung her head with abrupt, birdlike motions. Dimié Abrakasa averted his gaze, then pushed through the press of bodies till he got next to Baridom, the nearer of the two boys who he knew, and reached out a hand to tap his shoulder.

"Wetin the crazewoman do?" he asked.

Baripo, the second boy, threw Dimié Abrakasa an angry glance. "She *craze*," he said.

At that moment, the madwoman dropped her hands to the ground and pushed herself up. The boys, it seemed, were expecting this move: those holding sticks leaped forward and delivered blows to her head, her back, her buttocks, her legs. Shrieks of pain burst from her throat as she danced around to avoid her attackers, her movements as wild as a leaping flame. Then she sank back to her haunches.

The boys resumed their stargazing. This game was no longer play. They were drunk on high spirits. They fidgeted, impatient with the madwoman's cowardice. Some of the boys, whoops bursting from their throats, broke the ring to make short, darting runs at the hunched form.

Someone said: "If crazewoman bite you, you go craze." Nods and murmurs of agreement traveled the circle.

"If dog wey get rabies bite you, you go craze too," said Baripo.

"Yes o," Baridom agreed.

"Me, but before I craze, I go burst that dog head," said the boy who had spoken first.

"You no go fit," Baripo said. "Dog wey get rabies dey craze."

"I go fit."

"You no go fit."

"I say I go fit!"

"I say you no fit!"

The boy said: "I go fit burst *this* crazewoman head. Try me!"

Silence. Then the boys' voices rose in a chorus of cheers and jeers. "You no fit, Ériga—do am, Ériga—burst the crazewoman head!"

Ériga whirled to face Dimié Abrakasa, who was beside him. "You get stone?" Dimié Abrakasa shook his head no. Baripo asked: "You want stone?" Without waiting for a reply, Baridom held out a lump of brick. Dimié Abrakasa, who stood between Ériga and

Baridom, reached for the brick, closed his fist around it, hefted it, and then flung it at the madwoman. It struck the side of her head and disintegrated in a shower of dust. She screamed, horribly. It was this explosion of mingled pain and rage—and the superhuman force with which she leaped at her attackers, blood splashing from the gash in her head—that caused the boys to break rank and flee from the alley, their yells trailing in their wake.

₿ɔ

By the time the fear that combusted in his belly had been exhausted, Dimié Abrakasa was far from the alley, the boys, and the marketplace. He leaned against the rusting frame of an electrical pole and struggled to regain his breath. His chest heaved and fell. His hands clutched at his throat and clawed at the neck of his T-shirt, smudging the yellow. His eyes darted, searching for the pursuer who had laid grip of his imagination. Passersby slowed as they approached, shot him curious glances, and then hurried past.

· 5 ·

Dimié Abrakasa was back on Ernest Ikoli Road, at Railway Junction, when the rainclouds caught the sun. The world turned gray, the temperature plummeted, and gusts of wind sprang up. The wind grew stronger and flung dust into the air. A lightning flash split the gloom and a rumble of cascading boulders burst from the skies. Another flash, sulphuric in its intensity—the thunderclap was like a shredding of the heavens.

Birds crawled across the sky with panicked cries. There was a lull, everything froze in that instant; and then, with a sound like burning grass, rain fell. The raindrops had not made landfall when a bolt of blue-white lightning, like a forked tongue, streaked the sky, and one of its prongs struck a fleeing swallow. The bird stalled in midflight, then began to tumble earthward as the rain hit the ground.

Through sheets of crashing water, pedestrians sprinted for cover. Puddles formed on the sidewalks, then flowed together and rushed for the drains, which brimmed over and poured water onto the road. The road became a river. Car engines drank water, coughed out steam, and died. Both sides of the road—and the sidewalks, too—got jammed. The horn blares of motorists became one long, unbroken blast.

᠍

Dimié Abrakasa moved off the sidewalk onto the road and wove through the stalled cars. The bonnet of the Toyota Sequoia beside him was warm—the car was empty but the engine was running. The driver had alighted and rushed off to join the crowd that was gathered at the head of the traffic jam.

Dimié Abrakasa headed for the crowd and squeezed through the swarming bodies till he reached the front, where there was a large flooded pothole. The obstructed traffic was caused by a ramshackle, cattle-hauling lorry that had tried to charge across the pothole. The lorry was stuck. The lorry driver was on his knees in the tea-colored water, scooping handfuls of mud from under the lorry's tires. Water lapped against his chest.

Like wind in the treetops, loud voices swept through the crowd, arguing. Some urged that the lorry be pushed aside, and others recommended a detour round it. Dimié Abrakasa watched, fascinated, as the crowd split into factions and yelled in each other's faces. Two traffic wardens and a policeman stood in the crowd. One of the wardens gaped at the angry faces with his hands clasped behind his head, while the second man glared at the lorry, his features drawn into a scowl. The policeman tried to arbitrate contending views, but he was repaid for his efforts by getting sucked into a quarrel that grew so heated he had to flash his handcuffs to extricate himself.

From the edge of the crowd, someone yelled: "Thank God—the army has come!"

A column of soldiers approached at a trot, their bootheels drumming the road. The crowd parted before them, scrambling out of their path. When they arrived at the obstruction, their leader—a stocky, potbellied sergeant who bore on both cheeks the four slashes that was the mark of Egba nobility—bellowed, *"Qua Shun!"* The soldiers stood at attention. Each held a horsewhip in one hand and an assault rifle in the other. Twirling his whip as he turned to the crowd, the sergeant ordered, "All civilians clear the area, *now!*"

The crowd dispersed. There was a flurry of banging car doors.

The traffic wardens had fled, but the policeman stood his ground. Thrusting out his chest, he walked up to the army sergeant, who turned to face him, surprise written across his face.

"Sergeant, sah!" the policeman said, saluting, "the situation on ground—"

The sergeant interrupted him. "What situation?"

The policeman, who towered over the sergeant, leaned forward with a wide smile. "The lorry responsible for this wahala . . ."

"Are you a soldier?" the sergeant asked.

"No, sah, but—"

"Are you a retired soldier?"

"No, sah." The policeman began to fidget.

"Is your wife a soldier?"

"No!"

The policeman, glancing around at the column of stonefaced soldiers when he made his reply, did not see the twist of rage on the sergeant's face as he roared, "Bloody civilian!" and dealt the policeman a sledgehammer blow to the throat. The policeman fell to the ground, jerking as he fought to keep from swallowing his tongue. Grasping the fallen man by the collar, the sergeant slashed him across the face with his whip, then dragged him to the edge of the flooded pit, released him, and stepped back a pace. The sergeant's face regained its humanity.

"Roll in the mud, you shit," he said, calmly.

Trembling from fear and pain, and bleeding from the cut to his face, the policeman squeezed his eyes shut and crawled into the pool of muddy water. He lay down on his belly, bobbed for an instant, and then began to roll, the water rippling. The sergeant hung his whip round his neck and, with deliberate slowness, folded his sleeves. When he was done, he said, his voice barely above a whisper: "Out."

The policeman scrambled out of the water on all fours, gasping for air. The sergeant turned to his men and ordered, "Clear that lorry from the road."

The soldiers leaped into action. They beat up the lorry driver and then offloaded his cargo of cattle, which they sent galloping off with kicks to their rumps. Then they strode through the crowd, handpicking hefty men. The men pulled the lorry, and the soldiers pushed. The sergeant directed the traffic, his whip flailing as he yelled instructions. In a few minutes the cars were honking their thanks and speeding off.

⁂

The rain had stopped. Dimié Abrakasa was wet, hungry, and tired. He had been gone too long—Méneia and Benaebi would be waiting for him, maybe even now watching both ends of the street to see who would spot him first. Then his thoughts were interrupted by the sound of his name. He looked up and saw a sea of cars. *Dimi!* he heard again, above the noise of the engines. He saw the waving hand and recognized the car—a decrepit white Peugeot 404—and then the face of his landlord, Alhaji Tajudeen. The landlord was pushing the car with one hand and controlling the steering wheel with the other. The line of cars behind him honked at his slow progress. Dimié Abrakasa ran to help him.

"Afternoon, sir," he greeted. He moved to the back of the car. They pushed together. The car rolled faster.

"Can you push alone?" Alhaji Tajudeen asked, looking over his shoulder.

"Yes," Dimié Abrakasa answered.

"Okay." Alhaji Tajudeen jumped into the driver's seat and pulled the door shut.

"Push! Push!"

Dimié Abrakasa bit his lip; his feet scrabbled on the rain-slick tarmac.

"Come on, you're not a woman—*push!*"

The exhaust backfired with a blast of thick, white smoke. The engine caught, sputtered, and sparked into life. Dimié Abrakasa, his face shining with sweat, ran toward the passenger door. He was reaching for the handle when the car swerved into the hooting, fast-flowing traffic and sped off. Dimié Abrakasa stood clutching the air. And then he scrambled off the road.

· 6 ·

The outdoor bar had for shade an old beach umbrella, under which stood a table and a bench. Six men sat on the bench, three stood around the table. The men held beer tankards, whiskey glasses, plastic cups. Bottles of different sizes, shapes, and colors, arranged in no particular order but with a woman's eye for beauty, covered the table. The bar owner sat on the knee of one of her customers. The man's hands rested in her lap, and he tilted back his head to drink from the glass she held to his lips. When the woman saw Dimié Abrakasa approaching her stall, she thrust the glass into the man's hand, stood up, and walked forward.

"Wetin you want?" she said, as she planted herself in front of the boy. "Make you no think sey I go serve you drink o!"

The woman had a spoiled milk complexion, the reward for a lifetime regime of bleaching cream. Her knuckles were the color of healed bruises, her arms and legs were crisscrossed with thick blue veins. The deep brown of her unpainted lips made them seem sweet, coated with treacle, smudged with chocolate.

"Wetin you dey look, you no fit talk?" the woman asked angrily. She placed her hands on her hips, harassed Dimié Abrakasa with her gaze. He dropped his eyes.

One of the men on the bench gave a snort of a laugh. He called out: "Madam Glory, leave the small boy abeg."

Madam Glory spun round and pointed her finger at him. "Hear me, and hear me well—no put your rotten mouth for this one o! I no dey serve pikin for here. If this small boy wan' kill himself"—and here she turned to face Dimié Abrakasa, her forefinger stabbing—"make e find another person shed. No be my business Satan go use to spoil another woman pikin." She raised her hand, sketched a halo above her head, and then snapped her thumb and middle finger at Dimié Abrakasa. "I reject it in Jesus name!"

"Ah ah, Madam Glory, you sef!" exclaimed the man who had spoken. "You know whether somebody send the boy?"

"Even still," she said in a calmed voice. She stared at Dimié Abrakasa, her eyes sparking suspicion. "They send you?" she asked.

"Yes," Dimié Abrakasa said.

"Who send you?"

Dimié Abrakasa was about to say the truth, that he had been sent by his mother, when his right hand, which was tugging the hem of his T-shirt, crept into his trouser pocket. He pulled back the hand, stared at Madam Glory with horror, then dug both hands into his pockets, and gasped out:

"My God!"

"What!" Madam Glory cried. "You dey make joke with me?" Goaded by the guffaws that burst from the men behind her, she bore down on Dimié Abrakasa. She caught him by the earlobe just as he turned to flee, and dragged him forward, cursing under her breath, her face stained with rage. She reached the edge of the road, released his burning ear, and with a shove to his head she ordered: "Get away from here! Useless child, mumu, I sorry for your mama! Get away!"

ॐ

On the trek back to a house that loomed before him like a Golgotha, Dimié Abrakasa ransacked even the most protected corners of his memory for the missing money. Despair, at several points on his journey, almost made him break down in tears, but each time his will overcame that foolishness.

· 7 ·

Number II Sand Field was at the intersection of Yakubu Gowon and Adaka Boro Streets. It was one of eleven open spaces— Number IV Grass Field, Number VI Paved Field, Number VII Clay Field, Number X Sand Field, et cetera—set up all over Poteko by a past military administrator. Number II was a football pitch, with white sand instead of turf, and it was enclosed by a low concrete wall. On weekends when football matches between local clubs were staged in this arena, the wall disappeared under a swarm of spectators, but on this afternoon, as Dimié Abrakasa vaulted the wall, the field was deserted.

At one end of the field, in the space behind the goalpost, a table tennis board was set up. Three boys stood round the table, and two of them were engaged in a game. The ball flew into the net as Dimié Abrakasa drew up beside the table, and the third boy, who clutched a wad of naira notes in one hand, called out, "Park five!"

"Who dey win?" Dimié Abrakasa asked.

"*Sh!*" hissed the player whose turn it was to serve. He cast a furious look at Dimié Abrakasa. They recognized each other at the same instant.

"You!" Ériga exclaimed. "But how you dey? How you escape that crazewoman?"

The other player spoke. "This nah the boy you tell us about? The one wey stone the crazewoman?"

"Yes o!"

"Strong man—correct guy!" Three pairs of eyes gazed at Dimié Abrakasa with approbation. Then Ériga whirled round to face the table, and served the ball. His opponent was taken unawares: he scrambled for the ball: his bat struck it out of play.

"Game up!" the umpire announced, running to where the ball had fallen.

The second player glared at Ériga and snorted with annoyance. "Nah lie Chibuzo, I no agree—I never ready when Ériga serve the ball!" he said.

"But you no say *let*, Krotembo," Ériga said. "Anybody hear am say let?"

"No," Chibuzo said.

"But you rush me! You must replay!"

Ériga threw his bat on the table. "I don win," he said. He strode to the umpire and held out his hand. "Give me my money."

"No give Ériga that money o, Chibuzo," Krotembo said. He, too, tossed his bat on the table, and began to unbutton his shirt. "You must replay or we go cancel the betting. You no strong enough to cheat me."

The two boys drew up to each other, stood nose-to-nose, and exchanged glares. Krotembo, who was shorter, had muscles like a blacksmith's apprentice. He raised a clenched fist, nudged Ériga in the chest. "No try me, Ériga," he said.

Ériga stepped backward, lowered his gaze, spun round on the

ball of his left foot, and ran. Krotembo barked with laughter. He turned to Chibuzo, chuckling in his throat. Then he heard the crash of glass. From the corner of his eye he saw the shadow of death bearing down on him, and he bolted.

"Why you run?" Ériga yelled after him. He stopped beside the table, strutted back and forth, panting with anger and brandishing a broken bottle. "Come and fight—if you get power!"

Krotembo watched Ériga from a safe distance. His naked chest heaved noisily. Then he touched the tip of his forefinger to his tongue and bent down to scrape the earth with it. He pointed the finger at Ériga and said, in a voice that quavered: "I swear, Ériga, anywhere I see you, anywhere I catch you—"

"Sharrap there, buffoon!"

Krotembo pressed his fist to his lips. His arm shook, his forehead bulged with veins. Then he turned around and strode off. Ériga watched the receding figure until he was sure the retreat was not a trick. He walked to the table, tossed his weapon under it, then snatched up Krotembo's shirt from the table, wiped the sweat from his face and neck, and flung the shirt away. It sailed through the air, unfurling.

Chibuzo spoke. "Make sure you run any time you see Krotembo o—e no go forgive you. Anyhow, two of you bet one-eighty, so after I remove my cut, your money nah three-ten. Correct?"

Ériga nodded, and watched Dimié Abrakasa from the corner of his eye. Dimié Abrakasa caught his gaze, and he turned away, accepted the roll of notes from Chibuzo. After counting the money, he asked Dimié Abrakasa:

"You wan' play me betting?"

"Never!" Dimié Abrakasa replied.

Ériga threw back his head and laughed. "No fear, I no be Atanda Musa, why you no try your luck, maybe you go beat me." His eyes danced as he awaited a response. Then he said, "Anyway, since nobody want to play me, I don dey go."

Dimié Abrakasa shrugged. "Me too," he said.

As Chibuzo gathered the balls and bats, the two boys left together. They strode across the sandscape, their footsteps flopping, their progress marked by the leap-and-dance of their shadows.

∂

At the end of Yakubu Gowon Street loomed a pink, three-story building, a hotel. The wall around it was crowned with colored glass shards, and the yard was planted with a profusion of fruit-bearing trees. Near the gate a large false almond tree grew at an abnormal angle and leaned over the wall. Its foliage formed a thick shade on the outside of the fence.

The boys reached the fence, and Ériga walked under the tree shade, turned to face the road, sank into a crouch in the bed of dead leaves, and rested his shoulders against the wall. Dimié Abrakasa followed. A gentle breeze wafted the smell of decayed fruit into their faces. A moment of silence, during which the leaf dust stirred by their arrival sailed through the air, and then Ériga touched Dimié Abrakasa's shoulder, said, "Wetin be your name?"

"Dimié."

"Dimi. Dimi Craze . . . De Craze." Ériga nodded, pleased with himself. "I go call you De Craze. My name nah—"

"Ériga. I know."

Dimié Abrakasa trapped a wood ant crawling up his arm. He picked it off his skin and looked at the waving legs, the snapping pincers. He crushed it between his fingertips and wiped his hand on his jeans.

"Why you stone that crazewoman?" Ériga asked. His eyes were fixed on his companion's hand—the long, tapered fingers, the bitten-down nails, the network of fine veins.

Dimié Abrakasa noticed the direction of his gaze, and balled a fist. "Nothing," he replied. But the image rose in his mind of his mother sitting in bed with her knees drawn up and her hands pressed against her ears. His fist rose in the air and struck his knee twice, then he let his hand fall onto the carpet of leaves.

"You be strange person sha. De Craze," Ériga said.

The street grew busy with schoolchildren returning from extramural classes. A group of uniformed girls was headed toward the hotel. The girls whispered to each other and darted glances at the boys; as the group filed past, the girl who walked in front turned her head to stare at Ériga, and snorted with laughter.

Ériga sprang to his feet and bounced on the balls of his feet toward the girl. The girl was tall and stocky, she had the calves of a shot-putter, her hair was shaved to bristles, and she wore the one-piece dress of a high school junior. Her sole ornament was a rubber wristband that announced her loyalty to Chelsea FC. Ériga drew up alongside her, and asked in a rude, deepened voice, "Nah who you dey laugh, woman-man?" The whole group halted and faced him. He repeated his question, and the girls, as if on signal, broke into peals of laughter. They stamped their feet and clutched their bellies and bumped against each other. Ériga's face puckered with anger. He grabbed the wrist of the girl whom he'd addressed and twisted her arm, not too much, but enough to make her aware of his strength. "Laugh now," he said, and pulled her forward, trod on her foot.

The girls fanned out, encircling him, buzzing like disturbed bees. He felt the movement of his hostage, but thought nothing of it, until her fist sank into his belly. He released her arm and doubled over, mewling with agony.

"Are you crying?" the girl said, as she bent over him and clasped his shoulder in playacted sympathy. "Stand up—" her words were interrupted by a snigger, "if you can."

Gritting his teeth, Ériga straightened. The girls watched him and waited. He stood, undecided. Dimié Abrakasa stood up. "I know you," he said, addressing the girl who'd struck Ériga. "We used to go to the same school—you remember?—Saint Ignatius."

The girl stared at him. "You are Méneia's elder brother?"

"Yes."

"Ehen—so it is you! I was telling myself that I know your face." She stepped forward, bumping Ériga with her shoulder, and thrust out her hand for a handshake. Dimié Abrakasa took it. Her grip was firm. She kept hold of his hand. "Adafor is my name. Your own is . . . ah, I've forgotten."

"Dimié."

"Dimi! Yes, Dimi." She beamed at him. "I've come to your house before," her tone dropped, took on some hue, a bit of blue, "when your father died." Then her face brightened. "What school are you attending now?"

"GCSS Boys," Dimié Abrakasa said.

"I'm in Holy Rosary."

"I know."

"How?"

"You're wearing the uniform."

Adafor laughed, tugging at his hand as she swayed. Then she caught the smirk on Ériga's face, and her laughter stopped. She released Dimié Abrakasa's hand.

"This dude is your friend?" she asked.

"Yes," Dimié Abrakasa said.

Her nostrils flared with disapproval. She opened her mouth, but shut it without a sound, then looked at Ériga. "You will fall inside my trap another day." She turned back to Dimié Abrakasa. "Greet your sis for me."

As the girls' voices receded round the corner, Dimié Abrakasa asked, "How your stomach?"

"Okay," Ériga said. He took a step forward, then pulled up sharply and burst out: *"Girls!"*

Dimié Abrakasa laughed. "I agree with you, troublemakers. I get one for house."

"Forget them abeg. Hunger dey waya me—I wan' go find food."

At the mention of food, Dimié Abrakasa glanced over his shoulder in the direction of his street. "I have to go," he said.

"Oh, all right," Ériga said, and reached his hand into the waistline of his trousers. His hand emerged with a flash of blue, a Chelsea FC wristband. He slipped it around his wrist and admired the fit, then looked up and caught Dimié Abrakasa staring. He dropped his arm to his side and edged away.

"Hey!" Dimié Abrakasa called. Ériga halted.

Dimié Abrakasa recalled the moments of his meetings with Ériga: the request in the alley, the amount of the bet with Krotembo, the scuffle with Adafor. The disappearance of his money. Now it made sense. Random pieces fell together and a picture rose in his mind. Just like table tennis had served as bait for Krotembo, the baiting of the madwoman was the game that lured him into Ériga's trap. But of course. And the dare to stone her was the bet, the gambler's opening, the pickpocket's ploy. For Ériga, he was sure, was a pickpocket, a master thief.

His heart pounded in his head as he stared at Ériga. He was furious, as much with himself as at Ériga, and now that he felt a kinship with Krotembo his sympathy for the outsmarted boy grew to levels almost unbearable. Ériga was shameless and hardened in his ways—he had seen ample evidence in the episode with Krotembo. Yet he hoped. Maybe Ériga would do the right thing, given a chance.

"Erm," Dimié Abrakasa said, his voice a croak, saliva clinging to his teeth, "I fit borrow money from you?" The boys searched each other's faces. Dimié Abrakasa dropped his eyes. "Please," he said. "I lost my mother's money today."

Ériga's tone was curt. "I no get anything to give you."

Dimié Abrakasa nodded, and averted his face to hide the angry tears that wet his eyelashes. He turned, walked away, but after a few paces he glanced around. Ériga stood at the same spot, watching him.

"Bye-bye, De Craze," Ériga said softly, then whirled around and quick-stepped away, his arms swinging.

· 8 ·

Night was seeping in from the sky's edges when Dimié Abrakasa arrived at number 197. He met the landlord driving in. Alhaji Tajudeen stuck his head out the window and yelled, above the noise of the engine, "Wait there for me!"

Dimié Abrakasa watched the landlord park the car, wind up the windows, and lock the doors. The car panels were dented, rust-eaten. The windshield was spiderweb-cracked in the right-hand corner.

"Is your mother in?" Alhaji Tajudeen asked, twirling his car keys round his finger as he approached Dimié Abrakasa.

With a sinking feeling Dimié Abrakasa gazed into the land-lord's face. Alhaji Tajudeen had the widest nostrils he'd ever seen. They were choked with a jungle-growth of gray-brown hair, the same color as his ear tufts, which he left untrimmed even though his head was clean-shaven. There was only one reason the land-lord would want to see his mother. Dimié Abrakasa nodded the affirmative to his question, and then said, "But she's not feeling well."

The landlord was headed for the doorway. "Is that so?" he said over his shoulder. "That's nothing new. She hasn't been well for one day since you people moved into my house."

The landlord entered the corridor. Dimié Abrakasa marked his progress by the echo of his footsteps and the voices that rose in greeting at each apartment he passed. The sound of wood crashing against the wall startled him forward.

The door of their apartment was open. There was still no power: the figures in the room were outlined in shades of gloom. The land-lord stood over his mother, who sat at the bed's edge, her knees clamped together, her feet pressed on the floor. Méneia and Benaebi were huddled in the corner, beside the dresser.

"You and your children must leave my house today," the landlord was saying in a loud, hectoring tone. "For a whole three weeks your rent has expired and till today I'm still waiting? You think I'm running a charity here? You know how many people have been asking me for this room?" He paused to draw breath. "I'm telling you, if you can't afford to live like a human being, then live like a dog in the street. But you're leaving my house today!"

Benaebi snuffled. Méneia covered his mouth with her hand. Daoju Anabraba shifted her feet, rubbed her thighs with her hands, sighed deeply, and spoke.

"If we can just talk in private, please, Alhaji."

"Talk what? Talk money!"

"Okay, Alhaji. But let my children go—"

"What you mean, go where? Or don't your children live here too? Look, woman, somebody must answer for my money today. Whether it's your son o, or your daughter o, or you o, I don't care. All I know is that my rent must come out today or all of you will pack out!"

"But Alhaji, why are you talking to me like this?" Daoju Anabraba caught the fold of her wrapper, which was loosening, and tucked it under her arm. With the same hand she swiped the sweat from her face, and then rose to her feet. She was taller than the landlord; his head only reached her shoulder. One step and her breasts would push into his face.

The landlord stared at her. His gaze moved down, traveling over her body, chest to foot, and back up again. He cleared his throat. "Okay," he said, "I will respect you, if you respect yourself. But before we talk anything, do you have my money?"

"No. But if you just give me a few more days—"

The landlord sniffed with derision. "Your rent is already three weeks overdue. People are lining up for this room. I've heard that

you don't have a job—that you like to drink. I don't want any drunkard in my house, and a jobless one for that matter." He lowered his
voice. "So tell me, why should I wait?"

Daoju Anabraba was silent.

"I'm waiting for your answer, Mama Dimi."

Dimié Abrakasa tried to help his mother. "Please, Alhaji—"

"Shut up when your elders are talking," the landlord said, without looking at him.

Footsteps approached from the direction of the courtyard, then
hurried past the doorway of their apartment, and continued at a
sedate tattoo out of the building. It was the only sound in the house.

The landlord sighed. "I am not a wicked man," he said. "By
Allah's grace, I have children too. I don't want anybody to say
that I threw out a widow and her children from my house. That is
why"—he paused for effect—"that is why I will give you a chance
to pay the three weeks' rent that you owe me, *today.*" He held
Daoju Anabraba's gaze, and licked his lips, then lowered his hand
to adjust his trouser crotch, his expression pantomimic.

Daoju Anabraba got his meaning. Her eyes widened. "Ah, no,
Alhaji . . ."

The landlord shrugged. "We're both adults here. The matter is
in your hands." He rubbed his palms together with a washing mo-
tion and held them out. "It's your choice. Pay me my three weeks'
rent, today, or pack out of my house, today."

Daoju Anabraba sank down on the bed and bent her face to the
ground, her movements slow and heavy. Her hands lay in her lap;
she cracked her knuckles and tugged her thumbs. Her shoulders
flexed.

When she looked up at her first child and spoke, her voice was
firm. "Dimié, take your brother and sister and wait outside. Close
the door."

Dimié Abrakasa did not move.

"You heard me?"

"Yes, Mma."

"Get out!"

The children filed out of the room. In the gap between door and post, Dimié Abrakasa saw the landlord cross to the bed, and he heard him say, "Dimi is a good boy. He helped me push my car today."

ჵ

Footsteps padded up the corridor. Effusive good wishes, this time in farewell, marked the landlord's approach. When he appeared in the doorway, he halted and blinked at the full moon that bobbed in the night sky. His face gleamed in the moonlight. He yawned, then raised a hand to wipe his brow, dropped it to rub his belly, and let it fall to his side. He did not look at the children as he trudged to his car, unlocked it, started the engine, and drove away.

In the void left behind by the car's departure, Benaebi said, "I'm hungry." His stomach churned loudly as he sucked his thumb.

Méneia put her hand on Dimié Abrakasa's knee. "You spent a long time," she said. "We waited and waited, Mma was angry. What did you get?"

Dimié Abrakasa looked away.

"What did you buy?" she asked again.

The smells and sounds of cooking floated out of the corridor. A rat moved in creeps and bounds along the front wall of the house, heading for the open door, then sensed Dimié Abrakasa's stare and scuttled back into the shadows.

"Dimié!" Méneia cried, her voice trembling with alarm. "You got the thing for Mma, at least, didn't you?"

"I lost the money," Dimié Abrakasa said. He did not turn his head to see the expression on his sister's face. He knew it by heart.

Méneia stared at her older brother without speaking. Benaebi, with a wet moan, jumped to his feet and ran into the house. His complaints, high-pitched and teary, floated through the open door. At the scrape of approaching footsteps Méneia's grip on her brother's knee tightened. Then she removed her hand and drew away.

"You lost what?"

Dimié Abrakasa scrambled upright. His mother stood in the doorway. Where the moonlight touched her bare shoulders, they gleamed with sweat. Her movement, as she advanced on him, was brisk, vigorous, oiled with intent.

Her shadow swept over him as she pulled up, and her foot stubbed his right big toe. Bringing her face level with his, she repeated, "You lost what?" Her breath stank of old alcohol.

The blow came out of the dark. It hurled him off balance. Then she was on him—slapping, scratching, kicking. Dimié Abrakasa fell to his knees and buried his head in his arms. He received a mule kick in the belly that tore a gasp from his throat. When she lifted a concrete slab and rushed forward, the neighbors caught hold of her. She fought against their restraint, spewing curses.

A phalanx of neighbors bore Daoju Anabraba into the house. Another group of neighbors gathered round the hunkered down form of Dimié Abrakasa. Méneia knelt beside him, her shoulders shaking with sobs. Benaebi, awestruck at the ferocity of his mother's attack, was standing behind his brother, his hands clasped in his armpits. Mama Malachi, whose apartment was two doors down from theirs, touched Dimié Abrakasa's shoulder. "You have done something very bad to make your ma react like so," she said. Then she bent down, held his arms, pulled them away from his head. Someone switched on a torch and turned the light on him. His eyes were hare-caught-in-the-headlights bright. There was a speckle of blood on his lips and four flesh-white scratches on one side of his neck. As if in reaction to the light, blood welled from the wounds. Méneia caught her breath. Mama Malachi released his arms. They fell into his lap.

The neighbors drew to one side and consulted. A few words, repeated often, reached the children's hearing: words like *mother* and *landlord* and *drink*. Then Mr. Mogaji of apartment one—the first door on the right—approached them.

"Do you kids have somewhere you can spend the night?"

Méneia blew her nose. Dimié Abrakasa did not stir.

Mama Malachi shouted across to them. "Talk! Do you?"

Méneia coughed to clear her throat. "My granma's," she said.

"Go there with your brother tonight," Mr. Mogaji said. His torch-light played on Méneia's face. "Don't cry again, Méne, clean your eyes. We'll talk to your mother in the morning. I have some spirit and cotton wool. Come and take, so you can clean Dima's wound."

· 9 ·

Granma Anabraba's house was in a part of town notorious for its youth gangs. It used to be a good neighborhood, and the archi-tecture was a relic of safer times—the simple, cottagelike houses, wide frontages, and alleys that opened onto bordering streets. With fear had come a stack-up of security devices. Now, house doors and windows were reinforced with metal, front yards were walled and gated, and alley ends blocked off with piled debris.

When the Abrakasa children arrived at their grandmother's house, they had to rattle the gate for several minutes before a frail, frightened voice demanded: "What do you want?"

Méneia answered. "It's us, Granma."

"Méneia?"

"Yes, Granma."

"Dimié?"

"Granma."

"Benaebi?"

"Granma?"

"What are you children doing out so late? It's not safe! Wait, I'm coming."

The rattle of metal, then the front door creaked open to reveal a dark, empty entrance.

"*Psst!*"

"Granma?"

Their grandmother's voice floated across to them. "Dimié, look around and check if there's anyone near you."

The children peered up and down the street. "There's nobody, Granma," Dimié Abrakasa said.

"Make sure," her voice insisted.

Dimié Abrakasa stepped back and scanned the area. The street was deserted.

"I'm sure, Granma. No one is here."

Granma Anabraba appeared in the doorway. She paused there a moment, as if tasting the air, then she descended the short flight of steps and crossed the distance to the gate in a canter. "I'm coming, I'm coming," she whispered as she unlocked the gate, held it open for the children to enter, then clanged it shut and locked it. "Let's go inside, it's not safe out here," she said, herding them toward the doorway with raised, crucifixed arms.

After the door was bolted, Granma Anabraba bent down to increase the dying flame of the hurricane lamp that sat in the chair beside the door. She straightened up with a low groan, turned to face the children, and voiced the terror that had gripped her since she identified the noise at her gate as nothing less extraordinary than a visit from her grandchildren. "What has happened to your mother?" she asked, peering into Dimié Abrakasa's face. In the weak light cast by the lamp, she did not notice the scratches on his neck.

"Nothing, Granma," Dimié Abrakasa said. "It's just that we haven't eaten anything today and there's no food in the house. You know our Ben when he's hungry, he won't let anybody rest."

Granma Anabraba released her breath. "I was afraid!" she exclaimed. She reached out to draw her grandson to her breast, clung to him. "It's been so long since I saw you. You're too skinny, Dimié. Why don't you children visit me?"

Benaebi started to explain, "Mma said we shouldn't—" but Méneia cut him off. "Shut up, Benaebi."

With a bitter laugh, Granma Anabraba said, "Leave him alone. He's not saying anything I don't already know." She released Dimié Abrakasa and took Benaebi's arm. "Come, my child, let me feed you."

ℬↄ

When Granma Anabraba called from the kitchen for the children to collect their food, Benaebi jumped up from sleep and dashed down the unlit corridor. Méneia, before following, asked Dimié Abrakasa to let her bring him his food. He dropped back into his seat in answer. As his sister's footsteps faded, the gloom of the room washed over him, lapping against his wounds like seawater. He thought of his mother, alone in the house. She, too, hadn't eaten all day, hadn't gotten her drink, and she'd had to endure the landlord's insults. At the thought of the landlord, Dimié Abrakasa moaned. The patter of footsteps broke his reverie.

Granma Anabraba placed the hurricane lamp on the center table and settled into the seat across from Dimié Abrakasa. Benaebi, ignoring his grandmother's warning that he wait for the meal to cool, was already halfway through the food on his plate before his back had even touched his seat. It was yam pottage, one of his favorites, and it gave off billows of fragrant steam that made him pant and blow at every mouthful. Méneia handed Dimié Abrakasa his plate and sat down beside him. The scrape of cutlery filled the air.

Granma Anabraba noticed that her eldest grandchild was picking at his food. She asked, "What's wrong, Dimié?"

"Nothing," he said.

"But you're not eating."

"I'm not really that hungry."

Benaebi belched, stood up, placed his plate on the table, took a long drink of water, and flopped back into his chair. "More?" Granma Anabraba asked, but he replied, "I want to burst." He slapped his belly and groaned. His thumb—under the pretense of wiping the oil from his lips, then with a show of picking his teeth—crept into his mouth.

When Méneia finished, she collected the plates, including her older brother's, which he held out to her with a shake of his head when she made to bypass it. She headed for the kitchen, taking the light with her. In the darkness, Benaebi fell asleep. His breathing beat the air.

"Tomorrow is a school day," Granma Anabraba said. She enunciated each word as if she were talking to herself; then her voice shook itself awake. "You children have to rise extra early so you can get home before going to school. Méneia will sleep with me. You boys can sleep in your mother's old room."

Dimié Abrakasa stirred. "Granma?"

"Yes, Dimié?"

"I'm not sleeping here tonight. I'm going home."

"No way!" Granma Anabraba cried, jerking forward.

"I have to go," Dimié Abrakasa said. "Mma hasn't eaten all day. I have to take food to her. She's not feeling well."

"But it's past eleven, it's too late to go outside. No, no!"

"Mma hasn't eaten all day. And she's not well."

His tone ended the matter. Granma Anabraba hung her head. "But it's late. And the distance—" Dimié Abrakasa cut her off. "If you give me money for okada I'll reach home in twenty minutes."

When Méneia returned from the kitchen Granma Anabraba turned to her in one final effort. "Your brother wants to start heading for Adaka Boro this night."

Méneia placed the hurricane lamp on the table and adjusted the slant of its light so that it fell away from the look that was on her brother's face. "Are you sure, Dimié?" she asked.

"Yes."

She met her grandmother's bewildered gaze and shook her head. Granma Anabraba dropped her arms. They fell into her lap with a clap.

"Okay, Dimié, let me pack some food for Mma," Méneia said.

When Méneia reappeared with a plastic bag swinging in her hand, Granma Anabraba rose to meet her. She took the hurricane lamp, and, mumbling at each step about the foolishness of youth, she went into her room. When she returned, her bare feet scuffing the floor, she handed a fold of naira notes to Dimié Abrakasa. "For your transport. Plus a little something."

"Thank you, Granma." Dimié Abrakasa picked up the bag that Méneia had set down beside his chair. With his grandmother and sister following behind, he walked to the door.

"Hurry, it's not safe," Granma Anabraba said as she unlocked the door. Thrusting the keys at Méneia, she directed: "Follow him and open the gate. Remember to check before you open it, and lock it immediately after he passes." She placed a hand, gnarled and knobby like a mandrake root, on her grandson's shoulder blade. "Good night, my child. Greet your mother for me. Tell her . . . no, don't worry. Hurry now, hurry." She gave him a push, and her fingernails, for an instant, dug into the wounds on his neck.

· 10 ·

Dimié Abrakasa arrived to find the house asleep. The front door, because of the broken latch, was never locked. He pushed it open and stepped inside. The air in the corridor throbbed with the chirring of crickets, the scrape of rat feet, the philharmonic *croak-croak-croak* of toads. He walked to the door of his apartment, knocked once, and listened. He put his hand on the handle and turned it. The door opened.

The apartment was thick with darkness. He reached his hand

into the plastic bag and searched for the candle and box of matches he had bought on the way over. With the care of a mole in a burrow that smelled of snake, he headed for the redwood dresser. When he came up against it, he struck a match, touched the flame to the candlewick, poured melted wax onto the dresser top, and fixed the candle. The sallow, sputtering light fell on the photograph of his mother as a frocked child, perched on her father's knee, with her mother sitting alongside. His mother's eyes shone with the wonder of happiness. He turned around.

Daoju Anabraba sat at the head of the bed, watching him. Her arms rested on her knees; her hands dangled. Dimié Abrakasa stepped away from the dresser and moved to where he had left the bag. He drew out a stainless steel container and a bottle of colorless liquid. As the candlelight reflected off steel and glass, the bedsprings squealed. Holding out his offering, he approached the bed. His mother leaped down to meet him. She grabbed the bottle and sniffed its cap. "Dimié, my son," she said, her voice husky with tears. She kissed him on the forehead and cheeks—wet, slobbery kisses that slicked his skin. She took the container from his hand and placed it on the bed, then uncapped the bottle and threw back her head.

"Oh my son, my first, my only child, thank you!" she sang, and wriggled her hips in an impromptu dance before straightening up to clasp him in a hug.

Late into the night, while she nibbled the food and sucked the bottle, Daoju Anabraba apologized to her son, over and over again, for the life they were living, for her failure as a mother, for killing his grandfather. Dimié Abrakasa, a veteran of these episodes, kept his silence. Her speech grew slurred and slid farther into her throat; her eyelids sank, struggled, fell. She cried in sleep, the bottle clutched to her chest. She farted, loud and continuous. When her sobs became snores, Dimié Abrakasa rose from his seat at the foot of the bed. He freed the bottle from her grasp and placed it by the wall, where her hand, in the morning, would reach for it. Then he covered her up and blew out the light.

ℬ

In the morning, when Dimié Abrakasa opened his eyes, the bulb above his head was shimmering with light. He stared at it until black spots swirled in his vision; then he turned his head aside and found his mother awake. She lay on the edge of the bed, curled up like a dead pupa, her gaze fixed on his face. He greeted her but got no response. His heartbeats punched his chest and bile rushed into his throat, turning his mouth bitter. He rose from the floor and prepared to leave the house. He was spreading out his school clothes when she climbed down from the bed, downed the remains of the bottle, tossed it aside, and leaned toward him. She swayed and licked her lips—her inflammable breath washed over his face. Mother and son stared at each other. Her gaze was reptilian in its steadiness, and his eyes, luminous from despair, were the shape of a full circle. When Daoju Anabraba, a smile playing on her chapped lips, uttered the words, "I hate your eyes, my son," he slapped her.

Love Is Power, or Something Like That

When the clock on the wall behind the complaints counter struck 7:00, Eghobamien Adrawus swung his legs off the sofa and undid the laces of his undersized boots. He heaved a sigh as the left boot dropped to the floor. He stretched his arms wide and corkscrewed his torso, then froze and clamped his teeth but not quickly enough to shut out the zoo-cage smell that had been hovering just beyond his consciousness and was now lodged in the roof of his mouth. His gagging sounded like a broken suction pump. *Animals,* he thought, and spat out a blob of mucus.

The cell at the back of the station had come alive. The prisoners had broken into their morning chant; they howled for mercy and food and invoked God's retribution on the heads of their accusers. The stink of moving bowels wafted from within.

As his right boot fell with a thump, Eghobamien Adrawus yelled, "Sharrap before I come there!" and stamped his feet on the floor to give force to his threat. His face was a gargoyle mask of loathing.

A hush descended. It was short-lived. By the time Eghobamien Adrawus rose from the sofa, gathered his boots, and moved behind the counter to collect his rucksack, the walls of the station were reverberating with the prisoners' cries. He opened his bag and drew out a pair of slippers and a blue *adire* shirt. He stepped into the slippers, dropped his boots into the bag, and undid the first button on his uniform, then snatched his bag and shirt from the countertop and rushed for the door.

In the fresh air outside, he took a deep breath. A crowd of

prisoners' relatives—with their multicolored containers of food, their crumpled clothes, and their anxious, sleep-smeared faces— was gathered underneath the gmelina tree beside the gate. On the parade ground the duty inspector was leading a troop of men through the morning drill. The green-and-white flag flapped lazily as it ascended the flagpole.

Eghobamien Adrawus undid the second button. The cold tugged at the hairs on his chest. His fingers were busy with the third button when he looked up, attracted by the flurry of activity to his right, where the cars were parked. A door banged shut and the engine of one of the police vans coughed and started. At this sound, a column of policemen who'd been standing about, killing time checking their guns and the fastenings of their helmets and bulletproof vests, lined up and jumped into the back of the van, which then rolled toward the porch, where Eghobamien Adrawus stood watching. A Black Maria pulled out from the backmost row of the park and lurched into place behind the van.

The fourth button on Eghobamien Adrawus's uniform broke off and fell to the porch floor. He trapped it with his foot before it could roll out of range. He bent to pick it up, and straightened as the van stopped in front of him. Inspector Abacha was in the cab of the van, beside the driver.

"Morn, sah!" Eghobamien Adrawus saluted, drawing his feet together and thrusting out his chest. His shirt gaped open, exposing the slackened, sweat-browned neck of his fishnet singlet.

"Morning," the inspector replied. He leaned forward to look out the driver's window. "You dey live for Oyakhilome Barracks, not so?"

"Yes, sah!"

"Okay. We get operation near there, for barracks bus stop."

"Ah, wetin happen?"

"No worry, nothing serious. Nah just those bus drivers. We get report sey they are causing go-slow."

Eghobamien Adrawus nodded and stepped back.

"Enter motor," the inspector said. "Make we give you lift, abi?"

"Ah, thank you, oga!"

Eghobamien Adrawus pocketed the loose button and bundled his mufti into the rucksack. He buttoned up his uniform as he descended the porch steps; then he hurried to the back of the van and climbed in, and when he pounded on the roof, the van sped off with a blast of its horn, followed by the Black Maria.

℘

When the convoy, which now included three commandeered transport buses and two tow vans, arrived at the bus stop, the bus drivers and their hooligan cohorts scattered in flight, as they recognized from the battle gear and firearms that the police were serious. The policemen pumped their rifles, called out commands, and gave chase.

Though he was off duty and under no obligation to participate, Eghobamien Adrawus threw himself into the raid. He had just shoved a blubbering conductor boy into the Black Maria and was looking round to see where else he was needed, when he noticed a stealthy movement among a cluster of spectators gathered around some meat sellers' stalls. He stared at the group and began to jog toward them. The crowd held their ground until there was no question where the policeman was headed. Then they broke apart like startled bush fowl and exposed a man creeping on his hands and knees, trying to get away. The man, too, decided to run and jumped upright, but before he took a step Eghobamien Adrawus was upon him and tackled him to the ground. One of the policeman's slippers flew off from the impact.

"So you want to run, ehn?" he puffed, straddling the man's chest and holding on to his shirtfront. He dealt him a slap and then grabbed his waistband to pull him to his feet. The man was tall, taller than him, and so fair skinned that Eghobamien Adrawus felt a twinge of spite. He delivered another slap to ensure that the

man stayed cowed—he felt a coil of pleasure in his belly as he saw
the imprints of his fingers glow red on the man's cheek. He turned
and tried to drag the man away, but he was surprised to find him
resisting, not fearfully, pleadingly, but with unexpected force.

"Wetin I do?" the man protested, as he tried to prize loose the
policeman's grip on his waistband. The man's feet seemed rooted
to the ground, no matter how Eghobamien Adrawus tugged, he
would not budge.

"You dey resist arrest!" Eghobamien Adrawus threw a quick look
around. The other policemen were too busy to come to his aid, and
he could feel the man becoming bolder, less respectful. His fingers
began to slip—the success of the raid and the safety of his colleagues in that instant seemed vested in the grip of his fingers. He
released his hold on the man's trousers.

The man panted with triumph. He made a half turn to complete his escape, but Eghobamien Adrawus lunged forward and
flung his arms around him. When he tried to lift him off the
ground, the man gripped his shirt and locked legs with him. A
black, foaming fury rose to the policeman's throat. He glowered
past the man's shoulder at a table in one of the abandoned meat
stalls. A thin rivulet of blood flowed over the table's edge, pattering the ground.

Eghobamien Adrawus placed his lips against the man's sweat-
moistened cheek and snarled: "You dey challenge my authority—
you no dey fear?" The man's cheek muscles tensed, but he made
no reply.

Eghobamien Adrawus bunched his shoulders and strained backward, and when the man resisted, he heaved forward. The man
staggered back several steps and crashed into the table, bloody-
ing the seat of his trousers. Eghobamien Adrawus felt a surge of
power. He drove his knee upward, into the man's crotch. As the
man doubled over with a yelp, Eghobamien Adrawus released
his clasp on his shoulders and landed a blow on his mouth. The

man jackknifed to barracks attention, his eyes widening, his lips flapping loosely.

Eghobamien Adrawus took his time in selecting which part of the man's body to inflict punishment on. He punched him in the stomach, the neck, the ear, and when his arms tired, he head butted him in the mouth. The man began to chatter pleas, blood seeping from between his teeth. Eghobamien Adrawus aimed a kick at his legs, and with a shout, the man fell to the ground. Catching sight of the pile of butchered meat on the table surface, Eghobamien Adrawus reached out and grabbed a cow leg—the hoof dug him in the wrist and bloodstained ligaments extended like hacked wires from the knee joint. Wielding the leg like a truncheon, he clubbed the prostrate man over the head.

Someone in the crowd yelled: "You go kill am o!" The policeman, snorting from his exertions, straightened up. He scowled at the wall of faces. Through the unbuttoned part of his shirt his belly heaved like a hippopotamus in labor. The man on the ground moaned and struggled up onto one elbow, his shoulders trembling from the effort. One of his eyes was swollen shut and blood bubbled from his lips and nostrils. Eghobamien Adrawus tossed aside the cow leg and bent to help him to his feet.

"Come," he said. "You're under arrest."

ॐ

Overloaded with prisoners, the Black Maria turned onto the road, puffing clouds of smoke behind it. Eghobamien Adrawus collected his bag from the back of the police van and left the bus stop. His barrack was a short walk away but he had only one slipper. He had searched for the second but with no result. He flagged down a passing okada.

When the motorbike came to a stop in front of his apartment block, he climbed down and strode off without paying. The okada rider—a foul-smelling adolescent boy with mud-colored hair and arms as thin as cornstalks—released a stream of abuse at his back, his voice cracking with emotion. The invectives, delivered in a mishmash of dialects and mangled English, flew from his mouth with gobs of spittle. After the policeman entered the building, the boy swung his motorbike around and rode off with a shriek of tires.

℘

Estella was bent over the stove in the corridor. She looked up when a shadow fell across her cooking pot and, recognizing her husband, gave a cry, which was choked off before it could declare itself as fear or delight. She straightened up, wiping her hands on the front of her wrapper. Eghobamien Adrawus let her take his bag. He grunted a reply to her inquiry about his appetite, but feigned deafness when she observed that the neck of his singlet was stained with blood. He parted the curtain to enter the apartment, then halted at a dirty pot by the doorway.

"Nah Mama Adaobi pot," Estella said quickly.

"But this nah the second day."

"Ah Eghe, I don tell her make she remove am from my door-mot, but she no wan' hear!"

He glared at her for some seconds, then nodded and strode into the apartment. Estella followed, not wringing her hands, but looking like she felt the need to. The window blinds were drawn and the TV was on. He walked to the recliner opposite and, with a grunt, sank into it. His arms dangled over the sides.

"Remove your shirt make I hang am," Estella said.

She waited. His eyes were closed.

"Eghe . . ."

"Bring the remote," he said.

She walked to the TV and returned with the remote control. He raised his hand, wriggled his fingers to indicate that she hand it over, and closed his fist around it without opening his eyes. Pointing from the waist, he began to flip channels. The ashen, electrical light danced across his ebony skin.

"Your shirt, Eghe."

His eyes snapped open. "Sharrap woman, can't you see I'm busy?"

Estella wheeled round and strode into the bedroom. She tossed his bag in the corner and dropped onto the bed, disarranging the sheets and gripping her knees through her wrapper. She stared at the wall, her lips moving silently. Then she remembered the meal on the fire. She leaped up and rushed from the room.

Her husband was asleep. His mouth drooped open and a rope of saliva hung down to the steel insignia on his collar. Estella stood in the center of the room and watched the heave and fall of his chest, then walked up to him, sniffed his breath, and began to undo his buttons.

₭

It was Estella's voice that woke him up. He kicked away the bed-clothes and rose; he winced from the weight of his head. He walked to the bedroom door and pulled it open.

"You see—I told you the TV will wake your father. Oya, turn it off now!"

"Ah, Mummy—"

"*Now*, can't you hear?"

Estella was standing in the front doorway, with only her head and part of a shoulder visible through the parted curtain. As his nine-year-old son, Osamiro, shuffled toward the TV set, Eghobamien Adrawus leaped forward and grabbed the boy by the waist. He swept him into the air and whirled him around. Osamiro slapped his father on the head, then took hold of his ears. He shrieked with laughter when his father thrust his tongue into his belly button and made snorting, wallowing-pig noises.

"Me too, Daddy, me too!" said six-year-old Ododo, tugging at his father's underpants.

Eghobamien Adrawus allowed himself to be wrestled to the floor. He bellowed in mock pain when Osamiro, his thin knees straddling his belly, blew a gust of air into his ear. Clutching the struggling boy to his chest with one arm, he reached out and pulled Ododo into the fray.

Estella struggled to suppress a smile. "You men, I just arranged the house. I hope you will clean up after you finish this nonsense play?" Pulling back her head from the doorway, she asked: "Eghe—you don ready for your food?"

"Yes!" Eghobamien Adrawus gasped in reply, as he writhed under his sons' tickling fingers. Then: "Enough, enough! I surrender!"

"True?" Ododo queried, his hand still buried in his father's armpit.

"True," Eghobamien Adrawus said. "You win. Oya go . . . go and watch cartoon."

"Yay!" the boys yelled in unison. They sprang from their father's chest and raced for possession of the recliner and remote. Eghobamien Adrawus rose from the floor, arranging his Y-fronts.

Estella was stirring the contents of the pot on the stove. The steam from her cooking shrouded her scowl of concentration. "I dey warm am, e go soon ready," she said when her husband emerged from the apartment. He nodded and patted her on the rump. The neighbor's dirty pot was still festering beside the doorway. With cautious casualness, so that his wife wouldn't notice, he shuffled toward Mama Adaobi's door to check if she had returned, but as it was still padlocked, he strolled to the balcony for some air.

With his elbows on the balustrade, Eghobamien Adrawus gazed out over the chaos of Poteko City. Three floors below, the earth seemed to pull at him. The rooftops were a sea of rust, with the masts of an armada of sunken TVs jutting from it. The heads of passersby bobbed like buoys. Across the road, in a clump of goat-shit-green bushes, he noticed the splayed carcass of a dog. His gaze traveled and landed on the hive of activity that was the bus stop. The commercial buses were back, their overripe-banana color marking them out. When he heard footsteps behind him, he turned.

"Your food don ready," Estella said.

She gave off the smell of kerosene smoke, and a film of moisture lay on her skin. Despite long years of marriage, he still marvelled at her small size, her compactness. Her head, her neck, her arms, her feet, everything was molded in a way that overpowered him. As if she was made for a more perfect place.

"You say something?" Estella glanced up and caught her husband's eyes. "Eghe, no!" she said, backing away. "Make you eat first."

"No. I wan' eat you." He reached out to take her hand but she slapped him away. She spun round and strode toward the corridor, her hips swinging. He caught up with her in the doorway and clasped her by the waist.

"I want you, now, now, now." He tried to trap her mouth but his lips skidded off her cheek. She laughed and wriggled away. "The children—"

"Wetin happen to them?"

"If they see us—*Eghe!*"

He lifted her off her feet and threw her across his right shoulder. He pinned her kicking legs with one arm. "Make they see," he growled, smacking her upended bottom. "They go know sey their papa love their mama."

ॐ

With a groan, Eghobamien Adrawus rolled off his wife's belly. He turned onto his side and drew up his knees. His deep breathing melded with Estella's, and the room resonated with their contentment. Estella stretched out a hand and picked at the hair on his shoulders. The late afternoon sun streamed in through the open window, and bathed the room in an orange-red glow.

Estella exhaled. "That one good," she said.

"Mm."

"Nah that time again o, I fit get belleh." She paused. "Eghe, I wan' talk to you about something." No response. "About your uniform. I think sey we agree."

"I know, I know. I wear am because we get operation for barracks bus stop this morning. I no fit wear mufti follow my people, you know."

"Even still, I no want you to wear that uniform inside this house. You for don remove am before you come upstairs. Last week you wear am two times, this week you don start already. Small time now, the drinking go start again."

Eghobamien Adrawus sighed. "Okay, sah," he said.

"I serious o, Eghe."

The bed rocked as Eghobamien Adrawus turned to face his wife. Her left arm rested between them. The scar beneath her elbow, where the bone had torn through the skin, caught his eye. He averted his gaze. Her eyes were shut, her eyelids fluttering lightly. He noticed how time had left wrinkles around her eyes, creases on her forehead, and furrows beside her mouth, like a map of her life.

"Estella."

"Ehn?"

"Look at me, now."

He saw himself, in the depths of her eyes, the way she saw him. But he was distracted by the tic that had sprung up on her left eyelid, and when he returned his gaze to her eyes, he'd lost the vision: he saw only his reflection.

"Yes?"

The skin of her left eyelid quivered like there was a worm embedded in the flesh. He opened his mouth to speak, but desolation overwhelmed him. He coughed and thumped his chest with his fist, as if to shake something loose. When he recovered, Estella said, "I dey come, I wan' go baff." She rose from the bed, picked her wrapper up from the bedpost, threw it over her nakedness, and left the room.

Eghobamien Adrawus rolled onto his back. He glowered at the ceiling, chewing his lips, so immersed in the acid broth of his thoughts that he didn't hear his cell phone until the call was lost. When it rang a second time he rolled off the bed and, following the sound, rummaged through his clothes on the floor. The caller was his colleague, Chukwuma. The cell phone clock read 17:44. He'd missed the call again.

Estella emerged from the bathroom to the sounds of *Tales by Twilight*, the six o'clock kiddy TV show her children followed daily with the single-mindedness of mosquitoes. Their addiction to television was beginning to bother her; she would have to talk with their father about it. As she walked past the recliner, she said: "Osamiro, have you ironed your clothes for school?"

Osamiro ignored her. It was Ododo who answered. "*Sh*, Mummy." He wagged his head in annoyance. "Aunty Alaroye is talking!"

Yes, she would speak with their father, she decided, turning the handle of the bedroom door. "Eghe," she began, as the curtain fell into place behind her. But looking up to find her husband by the window, she caught her breath. Eghobamien Adrawus had put on his uniform. He was the picture of authority, the man in control; and he was staring at his open palm, his face scrunched up in fury. One of the buttons on his shirt was undone. When he looked up at her, she quivered, her hand rising as if to fend off a blow.

"Why you no sew my button?" he snarled at her. "You no see sey e don fall commot?"

She stammered. "I see am but, but—"

"But wetin?"

She searched so hard for the right answer that her head began to spin. But there was no right answer, only the truth. She had let her guard down. She had been diverted by his lovemaking, lulled by the mirage of normalcy. She had let herself lose sight of the apparition, the thing in black and battle-green that took over whenever he donned his uniform—that swaggered like it was drunk on authority.

"Sorry, Eghe." She hung her head. "I think sey you go wear another shirt."

Eghobamien Adrawus released his breath in a whoosh that beat Estella's nerves like wind from a dodged collision. "Wetin you dey wait for?" he said. "You no go come sew am?" He watched as she rushed to the dresser and bustled about it, searching for her sewing kit. When she approached him, needle in hand, he unclenched his fist and held the button out to her. "Do quick o, the patrol motor go soon reach here."

She dropped to her knees. As she raised her arm to hold the button in place, the fold of her wrapper loosened and the cloth fell to the floor. Naked, she began to sew, her fingers working like insect legs.

Eghobamien Adrawus tested the button for strength, then slipped it into its hole and smoothed the front of his shirt. "Where these people—" he said, but his words were interrupted by a horn blast. "They don come." He moved to the corner to pick up his rucksack and headed for the door, the thump of his boots rattling the dresser. He stopped in the doorway and turned to Estella: "Till tomorrow." He waited, as if he wanted to say something more, but then left without another word.

Estella listened for the children's voices through the closed door. Her life would continue where it had left off: she would make the children do their chores; she would visit the neighbors, chat, laugh, exchange gossip, then come home to cook, clean, watch TV, and sleep. She felt once again the mistress of her house, her destiny.

The room darkened: the sun had dipped behind a cloud. The marshland smell of night wafted in through the open window, fluttering the curtains.

Estella rose to her feet, picked up her wrapper, and covered herself. Then she threw open the bedroom door so the knob smacked against the wall, and pushed aside the equatorially patterned curtain. The children's heads whipped toward this explosion of sound, their eyes widening with fear at the look on their mother's face.

"Don't make me tell you again, Osamiro—turn off that TV!"

· 2 ·

With nightfall the five men in the cab of the police van grew silent—conversation, at this point, seemed like a dereliction of duty. The team had been assigned to patrol a section of the interstate route, but seeing as the night was too young to fritter away standing on the side of some deserted expressway, they had begun trawling the backstreets of the city, and spooled time with every detour and stop-off.

Constable Chukwuma, who was at the wheel, reached over and flicked on the car stereo: the blare of a saxophone filled the cab. Beside him, Inspector Habila let out a yawn. He took a pack of Rothmans from his breast pocket, shook a stick loose, placed it between his lips, and then leaned forward to kill the music.

"We near Havana Hotel," Mfonobong said, his words punctuated by the *krr-krr* of his fingers raking his crotch. The men on either side of him shifted in their seats—the whole station suspected that he was slowly losing his life to an intractable venereal disease, but in the observance of good form nobody said anything about his piss-colored eyes or the sores that festered between his knuckles. At least, not to his face.

Glancing to his side, Chukwuma said, "Make I stop?" Inspector Habila raised his hands in a gesture of prayer and muttered, "Okay." Then he added: "But make una no arrest anybody o, Madam Ruby done pay protection money." A tongue of fire spurted from between his cupped palms and sputtered out in a cloud of cigarette smoke.

Light and music spilled from the doorway of the long, low-roofed hotel building. The figures bobbing and swaying about the fringes melted away as soon as the car appeared. Its back doors swung open and three policemen emerged. Mfonobong headed for the entrance with long strides. Otizara and Eghobamien Adrawus followed.

Several groups sat drinking in the foyer of the hotel, their laughter vying with the boom of the music. The red bulb that hung from the ceiling turned everything in the room a comic-book monochrome. When the policemen appeared in the door-way, everybody froze in midsentence, midaction, like figures in an enchanted scene.

The scrape of furniture broke the spell. Madam Ruby, her enormous hips hemmed in by the arms of her chair, was strug-gling to rise.

Mfonobong leered at her. "Do small-small o, Madam Ruby, make you no for break the chair."

Madam Ruby jerked her hips free. She took a moment to re-arrange her skirt. "Hope no problem, officers?" she asked.

"Give me Gulder," Otizara answered. He dropped into a seat, unstrapped his gun, and placed it on the table. The barrel pointed at his chest.

"You nko?" Madam Ruby addressed the question to Eghobamien Adrawus, but it was Mfonobong who replied, "Adrawus no dey drink for duty." He grinned at her. "But you know wetin I want." He leaned forward and hooked an arm round her waist. His finger slipped beneath the band of her skirt. "*Kai!* But Madam Ruby, your waist nah one-in-town." Madam Ruby, with the grace of a bullfighter, spun away.

"Sit down," she said. "Make I serve your friend."

Mfonobong watched as she crossed to the freezer and stooped over it—her hindquarters formed the shape of a heart. He licked his lips, dropped his hand to his crotch. By the time she returned with a bottle of beer in one hand and a frosted mug in the other, he had moved to block her path to the table. She squeezed past, but as she leaned forward to open the bottle, he caught her wrist. "You know wetin I want," he muttered, his breath fluttering her long, burgundy braids. "Make we go inside."

Madam Ruby jerked her wrist free. "I no dey fuck police," she snapped, "not even for money." The bottle cap flew off with a pop.

Two of the customers, taking advantage of Mfonobong's moment of speechlessness, rose from their seats and fled the room. The others, not daring to draw attention to themselves, huddled over their tables and read their ill luck in the bottom of their beer mugs. Mfonobong drew away from Madam Ruby. "You prostitute, common ashewo," he spat. "Who you think sey you be?" His eyes glinted. "I fit arrest you now for . . . for running criminal establishment! When I throw you inside cell with those armed robber we go see whether you no go open yansh!"

Otizara gave a snort of laughter and banged his beer mug on the table. Madam Ruby spun round to face Eghobamien Adrawus. "Your oga dey outside?" she asked.

"Sharrap there!" Mfonobong snarled at her. "Who give you right to question officer? Insubordination, you cockroach!" But he made no move to intercept her as, with a hiss of disdain, she brushed past him and slipped from the room. "Imagine that buffoon," he growled, turning first to Eghobamien Adrawus, then Otizara. "Wetin she know about police? She think sey e easy to wear this uniform?"

Otizara gulped from his mug. Eghobamien Adrawus stared at the wall with a bored expression. His boots were hurting his feet.

"I no dey fuck police," Mfonobong mimicked, and puckered his face. "Okay now, we go see whether another ashewo no go fuck police!" He turned and dove into the corridor of the hotel, where the chalets were located. Otizara watched the beer in his mug froth and bubble as he refilled it from the bottle, and then he addressed

Eghobamien Adrawus: "Abeg follow Mfon," he said, "make e no put us for trouble."

Mfonobong stomped down the corridor, rattling the doorknobs. He had drawn his battery torch—whenever he burst open a door he pointed it like a sabre and hacked through the darkness. Eghobamien Adrawus followed some steps behind. As the door of the second-to-last room opened to the force of his kick, Mfonobong stopped. "Ah," he said, jabbing with his torchlight. Eghobamien Adrawus drew up behind him and looked past his shoulder. The room was furnished with a mattress and a wastepaper basket. Condom wrappers and flaccid streamers of tissue paper littered the cement floor. A naked couple sat side by side on the edge of the mattress. The man's face was bent to the ground and his hands cupped his groin. The woman stared into the torchlight, her features distorted by a fierce, cornered look. The room stank of petroleum jelly and mildewed plaster.

"Who are you?" the woman asked in a voice quavering between fear and anger.

"Sharrap there!" Mfonobong barked at her. He held the torchlight steady on her face, until she lowered her eyes. Then he swung it on her companion and ordered, "Remove your hand." The man raised his head, his teeth locked in a grin of pleading. "Remove am, you no dey hear? You want me to arrest you?" The man lifted his hands, then placed them on the bed beside his skinny haunches, and turned to the woman, sweat trickling from the corners of his eyes. Mfonobong gave a short, harsh laugh and moved the light to the woman's breasts. "Ashewo," he taunted, and dropped his hand to scratch his groin.

Eghobamien Adrawus leaned against the wall and jammed his hands into his trouser pockets. He looked at Mfonobong's back. He knew this game. He knew how it would end. He had watched this scene too many times. He no longer thought about interfering, so even the thrill he used to get from his power over fate—to stop it or let it happen, to save or not to save—was gone.

Mfonobong spoke. "You dey fuck police?"

"Ehn?" the woman said. Her hand crept toward the clothes on the bed.

"You hear me. Remove your hand from that cloth o, before I vex."

The woman folded her arms over her chest and clamped her thighs.

Mfonobong stepped forward. His shoulders filled the doorway. He unhooked his gun and fingered the breech, the sound loud in the small space. "I ask you whether you dey fuck police, ashewo?"

"I can't answer that—" the woman began, but fell silent when the man beside her grabbed her by the arm.

"Just say yes!" he hissed. When she compressed her lips in refusal, he whirled to the figure in the doorway and said, "Yes, oga, *yes!*"

Mfonobong glanced over his shoulder at Eghobamien Adrawus and creased his face in a wink. Advancing into the room, he said to the man:

"Get out."

"Thank you, thank you, thank you!" the man mumbled. He scooped his clothes from the bed, rose, and pushed his feet into his sandals. Keeping as far from Mfonobong as was possible in the tight space, he slid crabwise through the door.

The torchlight spotlit the woman's uncertainty. "I don't like this kind of thing," she said, but her words faded into silence when Eghobamien Adrawus, with a warning cough, stepped forward.

He placed his hand on the door handle. "Do quick o, make we dey go," he said to Mfonobong, who nodded as he uncinched his belt. With a final glance at the bewildered woman, Eghobamien Adrawus drew the door shut.

∽

The patrol team had been at the checkpoint for more than two hours, yet the men still had not wrung all the fun out of Mfonobong's description of his encounter with the prostitute. They blocked one lane of the outbound road with a cordon of

oil drums and tree trunks, and lit bonfires in the drums to an-
nounce their presence to highway robbers. They stood in a circle
round one of the drums, firelight playing on their faces, exagger-
ating their expressions. Inspector Habila had wangled a bottle of
schnapps from Madam Ruby. They passed this around.

"You for don see her face when the condom burst." This was
Mfonobong. His colleagues' laughter died in their throats. Inspector
Habila lowered the bottle from his lips and turned to stare at him.
"E burst?" he said.

"Mm-hm."

"You stop?"

"For wetin?" Mfonobong said with a chuckle. "E don already
happen, abi."

Eghobamien Adrawus gazed at the bushes on the side of the
road. He thought of his wife, his children, his home—he thought
how lucky they were. For some reason Mfonobong seemed intent
on destroying his family.

"Here, Adrawus, pass am."

He took the bottle from Inspector Habila and handed it to
Chukwuma, who raised it to his mouth. He felt how the warmth
of the liquor would spread through his throat, his chest; but his
imagination couldn't replicate the solid weight of good alcohol
hitting the belly. He'd made a pledge: no more, not when he was
in uniform. Not after the time he broke his wife's arm in two
places and had to accept her judgment when she blamed the reek
of his breath. She had laid down her ultimatum from the safety
of Mama Adaobi's doorway, and he, kneeling before her in his
underwear, hungover and full of remorse, had given his word.

Now he had to fight not to intercept the bottle when Chukwuma
held it out to Mfonobong. The pain in his feet drew his attention.
He sat on the road, unlaced his boots, kicked them away, picked
up his rifle, and rising, said, "I dey come, I wan' go piss."

The road flowed into the distance, a dual carriageway with two lanes in each direction, linking Poteko to the western delta, and onwards to the rest of Nigeria. It was divided by a strip of red earth that was overgrown in patches with elephant grass; and—in the section where the patrol team had set up their checkpoint—it was hemmed in on both sides by thick bushes and tall, wide-branched trees. From the bushes night sounds came: scrabbling noises in the undergrowth, predatory screeches and distressed squeals, the *sheesh* of breeze in the treetops.

Eghobamien Adrawus wandered so far down the road that his colleagues' voices faded, and the checkpoint bonfires became faint sparks in the night. He liked the feel of the tarmac, the hardness of it, against the soles of his feet. Several times, for no reason at all, he lifted his knee as high as it would go and stamped down. The rubbish of travelers lay scattered about his feet: a Styrofoam container upturned and seething with ants; a smashed Pepsi can; a half-eaten turkey leg. He crushed an empty crab shell underfoot, then halted and unzipped his fly. His urine sprayed into the bushes.

ॐ

"Adrawus! Nah you be that?"

The policemen peered into the darkness beyond which their firelight could not penetrate. Their rifle barrels threw long, wavering shadows against the road.

"Nah me o," Eghobamien Adrawus called back. He drew closer with slow steps, emerged from the shadows, and approached the barricade. His colleagues lowered their guns.

Eghobamien Adrawus saw a shimmer in the distance. It grew bolder, became a glint. By the time it collected into two halogen orbs that arced through the darkness, he and the other policemen had taken up their positions. Mfonobong flicked on his torch, stepped into the path of the vehicle, and waved the torchlight with the wrist motions of a fly fisherman. At what seemed the final moment, the car braked with a screech of tires. It stopped

within a hand's breadth of Mfonobong's knees. It was a black
Toyota Avensis with a customised plate that spelled "EGO-1."

"Sanu," the driver greeted Mfonobong, who'd walked up to his
window. Mfonobong remained silent. He trained his torchlight
on the man's face while Otizara circled the car, peering in. There
was someone in the backseat. Otizara nodded.

"Park well and open your boot," Mfonobong said.

The policemen made signs to each other with their hands. In
a flash they had drawn up the plan of action: Mfonobong and
Eghobamien Adrawus would do the talking while their colleagues
guarded the road behind and ahead. The inspector, as befitted his
status, would keep out of the discussion. Per routine, the inspector hurried over to the police van parked on the median strip and
climbed into the driver's seat, then turned on the ignition and
flicked the headlights to low beam, to show preparedness to give
chase. By the time the car pulled to the verge the game board was
set, the pieces all in place.

Mfonobong rapped the roof. "Off your engine and come out,"
he ordered the driver. A rush of chilled, Ambi Pur–scented air
spilled out of the car door as the driver stepped onto the road.
Smiling, he tossed a chunk of kola nut into his mouth. "My par-
ticulars," he said, extending a sheaf of papers to Mfonobong.

"I ask you?" Mfonobong said. From the other side Eghobamien
Adrawus asked, "Wetin dey your boot?"

The driver turned aside to spit. "Nothing," he said.

"Open am," Mfonobong said.

The driver's smile hardened. He locked eyes with the policeman.

"I say open your boot, you no dey hear?"

The driver turned his back on Mfonobong and stooped into the
open door to say something to the person in the car. There was an
electric hum as the right-side back window rolled down.

"Come here, Constable."

The authority in this new voice caused Mfonobong and Eghobamien Adrawus to start forward at the same time. The man's thick-muscled head was turned to the open window; his face wore no expression. He was dressed in a sugar-white lace dashiki, with elaborate gold embroidery around the neck and sleeves. His paunch was distinguished, his goatee assiduously trimmed, his eyes hidden by gold-rimmed sunglasses. His cloth cap lay at the other end of the seat, discarded among a jumble of newspapers. He exuded the fragrance of one who would think nothing of spending a police constable's salary on a bottle of cologne.

The light from Mfonobong's torch reflected off the sunglasses. "May I know you?" he asked.

"You may not. Remove that light from my face."

Mfonobong switched off the torch.

"So you're the one who wants to delay me?" the man in white asked, addressing Eghobamien Adrawus. His voice was deep and heavy grained. He spoke English like one who thought in it. "You want to check my trunk? What do you want to see?" He raised his voice: "Abdullahi—enter the car."

This command woke the policemen. "If you move!" Mfonobong growled at the driver and raised his gun. Eghobamien Adrawus rattled the handle, but the door was locked. "Open this door," he said. At that moment, right beside his ear, Mfonobong roared, "Come down!" and pointed his gun into the car.

"What? Constable, you dare point your weapon at me?" The man's surprise surprised the policemen—they exchanged baffled glances. Inspector Habila, who had come up behind them, interposed:

"I am the ranking officer here. Step out of the car and identify yourself."

"I am not coming down from this car . . . Inspector," said the man, reaching into the folds of his cloth as he spoke. "As for identification, here, take it." He extended his hand to Mfonobong, who lowered his rifle, leaned forward warily, and peered at the man's hand. He jerked to attention. Ducking his head, he reached his hand forward.

"Wetin be that?" Inspector Habila asked, craning his neck.

Awe had turned Mfonobong's rude baritone into a meow. "Nah bundle of five-five hundred o, oga," he said.

The inspector snapped his heels and stood to attention. "Thank you, sah—*ego one!*" he hollered.

"As you were, Inspector," the man in white said. His fingers stroked his belly; he settled back against the seat. "Abdullahi?" he called.

The driver entered the car. The engine started. The windows rose.

Eghobamien Adrawus tore his gaze from the money in Mfonobong's hand. The man's disregard for their authority was not believable. If he wasn't afraid, why did he part so easily with money, and so much of it?

Eghobamien Adrawus took a step forward. He looked back—the distance this put between him and the others made it harder to take the next step.

"Hold it!" he said. He placed his hand on the glass to halt its roll. "I still want to see what's inside your boot."

"Ehn?" Inspector Habila and Mfonobong burst out together.

"Yes," Eghobamien Adrawus said.

The light was too weak to show if his words had any effect on the man. And then it was too late: Inspector Habila darted forward and struck his hand from the glass. "Adrawus!" the inspector hissed, pulling him away. "Wetin dey worry you? You no get respect?"

"But oga—"

"No *but!* But which but dey for the matter—the oga don settle us, abi?" The inspector clutched Eghobamien Adrawus's forearm with one hand and threw the other round his shoulder, by turns massaging and slapping his neck. Their reflection in the closed window showed confusion on the inspector's face as he sought agreement from Mfonobong, who was nodding vigorously. "Settlement nah settlement. Leave the man make e go."

At the inspector's words, the car shot forward with such power that Chukwuma, who was guarding the road ahead, had time only to whip his head up and shout in fear before diving into the bushes.

· 3 ·

The policemen stayed awake through the night in celebration of their good fortune. At daybreak, after they had divided up the money, Inspector Habila insisted that they would drop Eghobamien Adrawus at home. In front of his apartment block, the inspector looked down at Eghobamien Adrawus's toes digging into the grass and muttered, "At least now you go fit buy the correct size of boot."

As he plodded up the stairs, Eghobamien Adrawus wondered where his weakness came from—was it the hunger gnawing his insides or the compunction that he still felt at the escape of the man in white, or maybe it was the beer that he'd shared with his colleagues. By the time he reached the landing of his floor, he knew it was not the alcohol.

He met Mama Adaobi on the balcony. She was herding a group of schoolchildren toward the stairs. He saw Osamiro first, then Ododo. He had not been aware, until now, that he owed her a debt of gratitude for dropping his children at school in her beat-up station wagon.

"Good morning, Daddy," Osamiro greeted, but made no move to approach his father. When Ododo looked up to find the path blocked by the figure in black and army green, he tried to hide behind Mama Adaobi.

Even though she was a friend of his wife's, that gave her no

right, no right, Eghobamien Adrawus thought. He glared at Mama
Adaobi until she looked up.

"You don remove your pot from my doormot?" he asked.

She stared at him with surprise. "Ah-ah, Papa Osas, you dey vex?"

"Just answer the question!" he snapped.

"I don remove am."

"Good." He stepped forward and dropped to his haunches before
his children. His hand shot out and caught Ododo by the waistband.
He pulled the reluctant child into his embrace, then shook him
back and forth until the boy burst into strained laughter. "Good,"
he repeated. He reached into his breast pocket and extracted a single
note from the roll of crisp five hundreds. To the ooh-ahs of the
other children, he tucked it into Osamiro's palm. "For you and your
brother. Don't tell Mummy," he said with a wink.

When he entered the apartment, Estella was slumped in the recliner. Her eyes were closed. The window blinds were open and
the TV was off. He stood in the center of the room, swaying. The
belch that had been gathering force in his belly for hours, ever
since he'd swallowed the first drink, erupted now. He raised his
hand to wipe his lips and his rucksack slipped off his shoulder.

Estella leaped up and stood facing him—her eyes watching
without blinking, the worm in her left eyelid wriggling.

"What is it?" she said.

"Nothing," he said, and he began to talk. He talked about the
anger that made him strike a man's face with the leg of a cow. He
talked about his too-tight boots and his sore feet, about the jail
smell that woke him in the mornings, about the fear on the face of
a woman who knows she will be raped. He talked about the man
in white who smelled like a pot of flowers and gave out money
like he was buying favors for the devil. He spoke so fast that spittle
sprayed from his lips, then so slow, so low that she had to bend
forward to catch the words. He was still talking as she took him
by the arm and led him to the recliner, as she leaned over him to

undo his buttons, as she stripped him to his underwear, her hands working with the sureness of routine. He talked till his voice became a murmur at the back of his throat. He talked himself to sleep. Then she folded his hands over his belly and rose to look down at him. She did not say anything. She did not have anything to say. Yet her gaze lay so heavy on him that when she finally turned away he smiled in his sleep, snuggled closer into the recliner, and said, "Good."

My Smelling Mouth Problem

I went to the dentist today for my smelling mouth problem and after the woman doctor said "Do ah!" she wrote something on her Yem-Kem notepad and told me I have halitosis. I nearly pissed inside my boxers when I heard that big word. I was sure it was one serious type of cancer. But when she told me that I should brush my teeth two times a day and eat fruit three times a day and drink plenty of water every day, I started to suspect that the English was too big for the thing that was doing me. So I asked her will it kill me. The woman looked at me like I was not a full-grown adult. But I was paying her money after all, and I know my right—so I asked her what does *halitosis* mean.

Smelling mouth. That's what it means.

So now, let me tell you the reason why I went to the dentist today.

Yesterday, after I finished doing what I was doing in school, I went to where I will enter BRT bus. In case you don't know, these are the new buses that the Lagos State governor imported brand-new from abroad. They are big and long like lorry, and they have their own special lane on the road, plus their own special bus stop, where there is no rushing and you must stand in queue. BRT buses are very popular. Why not? They are cheaper than danfo bus. Their body is still fresh, so therefore they will not tear your cloth. You must buy your ticket before you enter the bus and there is a bell inside that you will pull when you have reached your bus stop. The drivers and the conductors wear uniform and they are not riffraff. So you will save money and you will not be fighting with conductor to collect your change. You will not shout when you want to drop at your bus stop. No dirty conductor will take his smelling armpit and rub all over your face just because he is collecting his money. No drunkard driver will be driving speed like madman and will be cursing you when you tell him to take it easy. Also, in BRT, nobody will pick your pocket or touch your private part anyhow, not like in danfo, where they want to pack the whole of Lagos inside a fourteen-seater Toyota HiAce. So you see that there are many reasons why BRT buses are better than ordinary ones.

For me, the main reason why I only enter BRT bus is because of my smelling mouth problem. Every time I enter danfo, I must open my mouth. Whether it is to quarrel with the conductor for my change or it is to shout when the bus is passing my bus stop, I must open my mouth. And because they pack us like sardine, every time I open my mouth there is a problem. Even when I sit beside the window, it is still a problem. Either the person beside me will look me with bad eye, or the person at my back will say, "Who has messed?" or the whole bus will gather together and advise me to be brushing my teeth. I am sick and tired of this embarrassment. That is why I only enter BRT bus, where I don't have to open my mouth.

It has reached the time that I will describe myself so that you will know the kind of person I am.

I am from Poteko in the South-South, but I am right now based in Lagos because I am pursuing my OND at LASPOTECH. I am the last born of my mother, and this year April 13 will make me twenty-two years on the dot. In my looks, I am somehow hand-some and I am not too short. Also, I have muscles. Some of my Lagos friends are thinking that I have body because I used to do weight lifting before, but the real truth is, from the time I was small I used to follow my mother to her cocoyam farm—that is why I have muscles.

Anyhow, as I was telling you before, when I reached the BRT Park it was only air-conditioned buses that were remaining. (That is another good thing about BRT: some of them have air conditioners. But the bad thing is that the AC bus is more costly than the ones that don't have AC. Still yet, even with air conditioner, BRT is cheaper than danfo.) So I paid the extra sixty naira for the AC bus—it pained me, I won't lie—then I entered and selected one seat near the window. (There is no reason for me to be sitting near window in BRT, but I am used to it.) I was like the number seven person in the bus, so I knew I had to wait for long before the bus will full up. The driver had not put on the AC, so the bus was hot.

After small time, I opened the window for breeze to enter. I was feeling thirsty and I wanted to buy pure water from the hawkers, but I didn't see any small children. As I was looking, one fat man who was wearing KAI uniform started to stroll near the bus. Immediately my eyes saw him, my brain picked that it looks like KAI are starting to do their work, that these days when it is schooltime you will not see any small children that are selling things. This governor, the man is trying o. First LASTMA, then LAWMA, then LASAA, then BRT, and now Kick Against Indiscipline. All that is remaining for the man to give us in Eko is PAP—poverty alleviation program. After that one, he can go to Aso Rock.

Anyhow, as I was saying, there were no small children selling pure water. And me, I cannot buy anything from old mamas and young girls because of my smelling mouth problem. Those old mamas, they can give advice anyhow, and those young girls, they have bad mouth, they like to curse too much. But the small children, they will not talk when I open my mouth, they will just turn their face to one side.

As I could not buy pure water, and the heat was worrying me too much, I started to think that maybe I should listen to music to cool myself down. So then I brought out my phone and my earphones, and I put the earphones inside my ear. Dagrin died like two months ago and since that time his music is reigning, everybody is playing it, whether inside barbing salon or inside nightclub, whether big boys or street girls, all of them are playing his songs. So last week I went to Computer Village and copied his whole album into my Motorola. For like three days I have not listened to any song except the one that he sang with Omawumi, and somehow, even though I still like the song, I am sick and tired of it. So I started to listen to "Pon Pon Pon" again.

I got myself when the engine of the bus started. The air conditioner was on and the bus was full up. My ears were paining me. And also, the window near me was open. So I closed the window and removed the earphones from inside my ear, then I locked my phone and put it inside my pocket. After that, I raised my hand to adjust the air conditioner so that the chilled air would reach me well. When the bus started to move, I started to look outside, so that the old mama who was sitting on the same seat with me won't have any chance to start discussion.

Small time, we entered go slow. In case you don't know, this is a normal thing in Lagos, even now that we have LASTMA. The go slow was a bad one, but the air conditioner was blowing well, so me, I was okay. There was one fine yellow woman who was sitting on one of the seat at my back, who was talking to herself. She was saying that she was in trouble because of the go slow, that people were waiting for her at her shop and her phone battery was dead, so she could not call the people to tell them that she was coming. I felt pity for her. The woman was *fine*.

In fact, let me describe her so that you will know the kind of person she is.

Her skin is very yellow, like those Igbo albino that have black hair. But the woman is wearing a head scarf, so I suspect that she is Yoruba. Her nose is straight and very fine, and it has one small earring inside it. The earrings inside her ears are very big and also they are very flashy. She has two types, one is round like a bicycle tire and it is gold color, the other one has many ropes that are shining like decoration. She has red-color lipstick on her lips and she has blue-color eye shadow on her eyes. She is wearing a green-color satin top with short sleeves and also she is wearing very tight blue-color jeans. She is slim like a sisi, but her breasts are big and even as she is sitting down I can notice that her hips are big too. She did not paint her fingernails but her toenails are red like chicken blood.

Anyhow, our bus was moving slowly but surely—LASTMA officials were controlling the go slow. As I was thinking to myself how everything is going on well, something happened. The air conditioner went off. At first, I was thinking that it was only for a short time, and the other passengers were thinking the same thing too, because nobody was saying anything. But after like ten minutes the bus started to get hot like the inside of iron container, and people started to grumble small-small. Me, I just kept quiet, because if I open my mouth in that hot place, it is me that will be responsible for anything that will happen.

After small time, I opened my window, because all over the whole bus other people were opening their window. I was sweating. The old mama beside me was sweating. Everybody was sweating. Thirstiness started to worry me again. My condition was so bad that I started to wonder how bad it will be if I had made mistake to enter danfo. Joy gripped me when I thought about all the things I was enduring in the past, inside those iron coffins that those wicked NURTW people are agreeing to register as transport bus. Inside my mind, I started to praise Lagos State governor. If only our president had sense like him, maybe Nigeria will not be where it is.

Suddenly, somebody near me was complaining. It was a man whose voice resembled soldier. Let me describe him so that you will know the kind of person he is.

His head is shining because he has scraped off all his hair. His neck is thick like a cow's own. He is very tall and very huge and his skin is a chocolate color. The whole of his skin is shining like he has rubbed Vaseline. He is wearing a blue-color native and his sandal is pure leather (I have not seen the design before, so it is not the cheap type that you can buy under Oshodi Bridge). I am suspecting that he is a Muslim, because his feet are clean, there is no dust on them, and it is afternoon time. The way the man's skin is shining shows evidence that he has money. His voice is very deep, like baritone, so I am suspecting that he will have a bad temper. But I just like the man—he makes me to remember Mr. Kosoko, my social studies teacher when I was in primary five.

Anyhow, this was the man that was complaining. He was shouting that the driver should put on the AC, that we paid extra sixty naira so therefore we must enjoy it. The driver did not do like he heard the man. Maybe it was because we were sitting at the back of the bus, or maybe it was because the bus radio was on and it was singing Fela's "Confusion" at very high volume. So then, the man was raising his voice, and other people started to support him. All the time this trouble was going on, we were inside standstill go slow and the inside of the bus was like it was catching fire.

By now, all over the whole bus, people were saying that the driver must put on the AC. Then the Mr. Kosoko man started to get very angry. He was shouting that BRT bus is government motor; that no driver can be oppressing us with a motor that is not his own; that if the AC is not working then the driver should refund us back our sixty naira or he should take us back to the park so that we can enter another bus that has AC that is working. All the passengers, all over the whole bus, all of them agreed with him. So they started to shout, "Take us back!"

That yellow fine woman who was sitting near me, she did not talk all the whole time this trouble was going on. But immediately the other people started to say that we should go back, the woman shouted, "No o!" She was sitting on the seat at the back of the Mr. Kosoko man, and after she shouted no, the man turned round to look at her. He wanted to curse her but when he saw that she was very fine, he did not say anything again. But all the other people were shouting at her, they were saying that didn't we pay extra sixty naira for the AC, that why is she causing confusion, that it is because of people like her that our country is bad.

There was one man that was wearing a black suit. He was sitting at the extreme back of the bus. The man was sweating like a Christmas goat. The man and the yellow fine woman started to have argument with each other.

"Why are you saying that we should not go back?" the black suit man was asking her.

"It is unfair! Can't you see the hold up? By the time we go back and come back to enter this hold up again, time has gone!"

"But shouldn't we stand up for our rights?"

"Look, oga, you're talking English. Is it today that you want to fight for your right? Go and quarrel with police or even with politician, if you want your right. The AC that spoilt is not the driver's fault!"

"I am not saying that the spoiled AC is the driver's fault, but I will stand on my right. I have the right to demand that I get the service I paid for. Or at least a refund."

"Sorry o, oga activist, since you don't have anything better to do than to be fighting BRT driver. But me, I have people waiting for me at my shop, I can't afford to be wasting time because of nonsense AC. If you like AC so much, why not go and buy your own motor and put AC inside?"

"Whether I have a car or not is none of your business. What I am saying is that all of us paid extra sixty naira for the AC, and so we have the right to demand it."

"Oya, go and demand for it," the yellow fine woman said. Then she raised her voice higher than everybody's own. "Driver, don't turn back o! Don't listen to them. Carry go!"

I was looking at the Mr. Kosoko man when the yellow fine woman and the black suit man were quarrelling. After the woman shouted at the driver, the Mr. Kosoko man could not endure any more. He turned his face to be looking at me too, but he was talking to the yellow fine woman.

"Madam, why do you want to fight against all of us? Can't you see that everybody wants to go back? Is it because of your own selfish reason that you want to prove obstruction to justice?"

The yellow fine woman faced him. "Yes, I am selfish, I agree! As if what you're doing is not selfish too. Or you think it is everybody that wants to go back?"

"But you're the only one who is against us. Everybody is saying that we should go back—you're the only one who is causing opposition. You're not more important than everybody o."

"I'm not the only one! Other people are afraid to talk!" After she said this one, the yellow fine woman raised her voice so that it will reach all the other people inside the bus. "See this hold up, if we go back we will still come back to meet it here. And those BRT people will not even change the bus for us. They will just give us back our money and tell us to go and join queue again. If you agree with me that we should not go back, abeg raise your hand."

Everybody inside the bus kept quiet and all of them were turning to look at each other. After small time, only two people raised their hand. One of them was the old mama who was sitting on the same seat with me. The other person was one bobo in brown-color T-shirt who was sitting on the same seat with the yellow fine woman. No other person raised their hand.

"You see," said the Mr. Kosoko man, "you people are the minority. It is all of us against only three of you. Even if we are practicing democracy, we are still the winners. Driver, the people have spoken. If you don't want trouble, take us back!"

"Don't go back o, driver!" the yellow fine woman shouted. "Don't mind them, it is you that is driving, just ignore all of them!"

So the quarrel started again and the yellow fine woman—to tell you the truth, that woman has sharp mouth—was facing everybody. Me, I was just enjoying myself. It is true that I wanted to talk, I wanted to tell the yellow fine woman that it is not only because of AC that we are fighting, that if we don't stand up for our right then BRT bus will become like danfo too and they will be taking us for granted and treating us anyhow, but because of my smelling mouth problem, I could not say anything. Then the bus started to move again. Small time, we reached the end of the road where if the bus turns right then we are continuing the journey, but if it turns left then we are going back. The bus turned left.

"Yeepa!" the yellow fine woman shouted. She put her hand on top of her head and started to scatter her head scarf. "Driver, so you're going back? Mo gbe o—you have killed me! Ah!"

After she shouted, the Mr. Kosoko man turned round to look at her. By now she had removed her hand from on top of her head and she was using it to be slapping her lap. The Mr. Kosoko man stretched his hand to hold her hand, and he was rubbing the back of her hand softly, so that she will not be angry. "Don't worry dear, take it easy, it is all right," he was telling her, "we will not waste any time, you will see. Let me give my phone—you can use it to call the people that are waiting for you."

True-true, the Mr. Kosoko man gave her his phone, and the yellow fine woman did not complain again. Small time, the two of them were laughing like they knew each other before.

☙

When we reached the BRT park, people started to stand up and rush out before the bus has even stopped. Me, I was thinking that, see this people, what are they rushing for—the BRT people will put all of us inside another bus that is the same size, so everybody will surely get a seat. Anyhow, because I did not rush with them, I was the last person to drop from the bus. The driver was standing beside the door. He was talking to everybody as they were coming down. When it was my turn to drop, he was saying to me, "I'm sorry for the trouble, sir, the AC was working before, don't worry about your ticket, please don't be angry." Wonders shall never end. You see why I only enter BRT bus?

Why not I quickly describe the driver so that you will know the kind of person he is?

He is tall a bit and his face is rough, like he used to have chicken-pox before. He is wearing the sky-blue-color shirt and dark-blue-color trouser that is the uniform of BRT staff, but his own is ironed well, not like some of them. From the way he is smiling I can see that his children will be jumping up and down and shouting "Daddy oyoyo!" anytime he comes back to his house from work. In short, he is a good man.

Anyhow, when I reached the new bus that the BRT people had brought for us, the door was blocked because people were struggling to enter. The conductor was standing inside and he was shouting, "Don't rush o—there are forty-nine of you and all of you will get seats!" but nobody was hearing him, young man, old woman, small children even, all of them were just rushing like it was a competition. Me, I just waited till everybody entered, before I entered.

I couldn't believe it—the seats were full up! The conductor walked round the whole bus checking for empty seat, but everything was full up. So he came back to where I was standing and started to harass me.

"Are you sure you were in the other bus?"

Me, I just nodded.

"Who did you sit beside?"

I was using my eye to look for the old mama, but I didn't see her. So I wanted to go to the front of the bus to look for her, but the conductor held my hand. By this time I had started to vex. Why will our people be cheating like this? Everything was going on well until somebody came to sit on my seat.

So then I pushed the conductor's hand and I wanted to pass him to go and look for the old mama, but people started to complain. They started saying that I should talk now, that am I deaf and dumb, that why am I wasting their time, that the conductor should not fear my muscle, that all of them will gather and beat me if I touch him, that he should push me outside! As everybody was standing up and looking at me like I am a thief, all of a sudden my eyes saw the old mama. She was sitting at the extreme front of the bus.

So I shouted at the conductor, "See the woman I was sitting near! She is in front."

As soon as I opened my mouth, everybody closed their mouth. Even though BRT bus is long—with forty-nine passengers, I did not know that before—yet in the front, people were making *foon-foon* sounds and covering their nose. The conductor squeezed his face like I have killed his mother. Then he released my hand and ran to the front, and the bus started to move.

So therefore, the whole long journey I have to be standing and taking advice from everybody about my smelling mouth problem. It wasn't easy o, forty-nine people against only me. Those people, they nearly killed me with advice, I swear to God. And anytime I wanted to explain, they will just be shouting that I should shut up. Anyhow, to cut short long story, by the time I reached my bus stop they have analyzed the whole of my life and they have told me all the things that are causing my smelling mouth problem. So that is the reason why I went to the dentist today.

Trophy

The first time I met him I shook his hand and nodded when he told me his name, told me about his job and how happy he was to meet me. I had just arrived in the town. It had been a long journey: I was road-grimy, irritable, and looking forward to sleep. I got down from the hired car and a small group of men standing in front of my hotel lobby rushed forward, calling my name. They closed around me, all smiles and jabbing hands and drumming voices, new faces and names. He was with them, a man of medium height—maybe five-eight, same as me—with skin the color of rotted wood. On both cheeks he had tiger-claw scars: long, deep, in quadruplet. I wondered if his tribal marks were the reason his smile was shy, wondered if I would ever meet him again. When he said his name I nodded and looked interested, but did not repeat it, did not memorize it, so his name, like him, the person, the face, was forgotten.

I woke up the next morning feeling refreshed. After a big breakfast in my room I went downstairs to the hotel lobby to meet the president, vice president, public relations officer, and treasurer of Frontrunners Club. These four were the leaders of the men's social club that had invited me to run a five-day leadership workshop for its members. In my first seminar later that morning I introduced myself to the class, learned the names of my thirty-three students, and talked about my accomplishments. My opening address took longer than I had planned, and the signal for lunchtime—the president's mobile phone alarm—interrupted me. The class resumed from the one-hour break one hour later. Despite grumbles from the students, I stuck to my lesson notes, I touched on every point I had put to paper. It was early evening by the time I finished, and my throat itched from talking. I needed a beer.

I stopped at the open-air bar opposite my hotel building. Whenever I drank beer, I chose Star. I'd placed my order with the bartender—she wore a short flared skirt, pretty, and she had a cushiony behind, strong calves, small-boned feet—and I was waiting for her to return with my drink so I could crack a joke to soften her up, maybe ask for her mobile phone number, when I felt a hand on my shoulder. I looked up. The name, Babasegun, did not mean anything to me. I did not recognise the face. At the expression on my face, his smile slipped, he dropped his hand. "I was part of the welcoming committee that met you at your hotel yesterday."

"Oh, yes," I said, remembering. "You're the secondary school teacher."

He nodded yes, and stood his ground, so I asked him to sit.

"Thank you, sir," he said. He walked to a nearby table, picked up a plastic chair, brought it over, set it down, and sat facing me. I extended my hand; his grip was bold.

"Call me Iggy," I said.

The bartender returned without my beer. She stood by my left shoulder, her hip brushing my elbow. The bar had run out of Star, she said.

"Bring two bottles of Trophy," Babasegun said.

She walked away, her bottom rolling. "Is Trophy a beer?" I asked.

"Yes, our local brand. They brew it not far from here. It's cheaper than all those big-name beers. It's strong, it's for tough men. And it's low in sugar, so it won't give you piles. Try it once and you'll never go back." He paused. I glanced at him, caught his gaze swinging away. "You like women," he said.

"Who doesn't?"

He flicked his bright pink tongue over his lips. "How long will you be in town?"

"Four days. But shouldn't you know that already?"

"No," he said, shaking his head. "I'm not a member of Frontrunners Club. I used to be, but not anymore. I only came to show support yesterday. I don't know the details of your program."

Seconds after he finished speaking there was a low, vibrating sound, and a square of light shone in his breast pocket. Then the phone rang. The ringtone was a Tupac song I loved, a song I had learned by heart maybe twelve, thirteen years ago. At the time I was in my second year of university. I was a shave-my-head, pierce-my-nose, hate-the-East-Coast-and-Biggie 2pac fan. I was still with Comfort, my first girlfriend. I used to rap the song to her, chopping the air with my hands, playacting my martyred hero. These days, whenever I listened to rap, I chose Kanye West. Comfort was now a married woman with two children. Yet the memories flooded in like a sugar rush, floating on that unforgettable tune.

Babasegun pulled out the phone, glanced at the screen, cut the call.

"*Still I Rise*. Brilliant song," I said.

He looked at me, smile spreading across his features. "You like Tupac?"

The phone rang again. On impulse I sat forward, raised my hands in front of my face, and shaped my palms into blades. Karate chopping the air, I rapped along.

> *Somebody wake me I'm dreaming, I started as a seed the semen*
> *Swimming upstream, planted in the womb while screaming . . .*

Babasegun joined in, eyes wide, teeth glinting. Our voices rang out in unison.

> *On the top, was my pops, my momma screaming stop*
> *From a single drop, this is what they got—*

The call ended, the song stopped. I tried to keep a straight face but my teeth kept pushing through my lips. I wanted the phone to ring again.

"So," I said into the silence. "Now you know. I love Tupac."

"My man!" Babasegun said in a drawling, mock-Yankee tone, and raised his right hand, fingers spread in a West Coast W.

As we talked I saw him clearer. He wore open leather sandals, neat blue jeans, and a white T-shirt with "Mombasa" stamped on the front in red letters. He told me about his wife and three sons aged eight, six, and three. About his father, who died of lung cancer the same month his twelfth grandchild—Babasegun's first son—was born. Who left behind seven widows and a reputation for hard partying that was unsurpassed in the town.

The bartender returned with our drinks and two glasses in a tray. She set the tray on the table, placed the bottles in front of us, and arranged the glasses. She bent forward to uncap his beer. Frost escaped from the bottle's mouth. She grasped my bottle by the neck. "Wait," Babasegun said.

She looked at him. So did I.

"Iggy, this is Wunmi. She's new in town. She just came three weeks ago. If I wasn't married, there would have been trouble o. Wunmi is a very nice girl."

"And pretty too," I said, grinning at her.

"Hear me, Wunmi." He held her gaze, his face stern. "Iggy is a special guest, a VIP from Poteko. He has come to do important work here. Treat him well, make him feel at home. I want the two of you to be good friends." He switched to Yoruba. Something he said made the bartender clench her dark, full lips. She threw a sideways glance at me and said, "Welcome, sah." She uncapped my beer, picked up the tray, flounced away. I watched her go.

"If you want to fuck her, the ball is now in your court," Babasegun said.

℈

He owned a car, an old boxy Saab. Gray, rain-colored, upholstered in black vinyl. The tape player was a museum piece: the dials were Soviet-era utilitarian, and its sound was tinny, elemental. The glove compartment was crammed full of audio cassettes. He leaned across to pop it open, dug his hand into the pile, drew out several cassettes, and examined them under the screen light of his Samsung phone. "I have many, many Tupac songs," he said, and belched.

To the sound track of nostalgia, he drove across the road, through the gate of my hotel, and stopped in front of the lobby, where we agreed he would pick me up the next day at seven.

ꝏ

"Communication Tools in Leadership" was a topic I planned to finish in three hours, but my seminar ran on for five and a half hours. This time it wasn't my fault: many of the club members couldn't spell words younger than they—Tumblr, hacktivist, phish—so I had to teach some basic Web lingo. Several times during the seminar I calmed myself with the thought of the handsome fee I would collect at the end, and the bargirl with pretty feet, the move I intended to make on her tonight.

The class dispersed at nine minutes to six, and I walked the short distance to my hotel. I got to my room to find that there was no power, and I needed hot water for my shower, so I spent another hour in the hotel manager's office trying to convince him to switch on the generator, which he finally agreed to. I was on my knees in the bathtub shaving my buttocks when my room phone rang. I rinsed off and hurried out of the bathroom to pick the call. The receptionist announced Babasegun.

"Send him up," I said, then dropped the receiver, crossed to the room door to unlock it, and tiptoed into the bathroom, dripping soapsuds.

When I re-emerged, he was sitting in a straight-backed chair in front of the TV, which showed Al Jazeera. A redhead with a British accent was talking about Israel in a war correspondent's voice, and spread out behind her, a polite distance away, kept in line by an unseen cordon, was a crowd of chanting, gesticulating Arabs.

"Israel has bombed Gaza again," Babasegun said.

"No politics, I need to relax—had a long day," I said. "Beer plus a woman is all I want."

I picked up my boxer shorts from the heap of clothes on the bed. I put them on and dropped my towel. My skin lotion and antiperspirant roll-on were beside the TV on the fridge. I asked Babasegun to toss the lotion.

He rose from the chair, reached for the lotion, glanced at me. "Only women and sissies rub cream." He underhanded the lotion bottle to me, an amused expression on his war-mask face.

I ignored his bait, which I found offensive, too familiar too soon. I put on my chinos trousers, drew on my white linen short-sleeves, then walked to the fridge, picked up the roll-on, and smeared my armpits. While I snapped the buttons on my shirt closed, he walked toward the door.

The Saab stood alone in the hotel parking lot. Without a word we entered, Babasegun started the engine, drove through the hotel gateway, and swung the car right. I turned to him in surprise. This was the road into town.

"Are we going somewhere else?"

"Yes," he said, eyes on the road.

"What about Wunmi? I wanted to talk to her today!"

"Don't worry, there's time for that. But first you need to see more of my town."

༄

The new place had an open-sided pavilion in front, where we sat. At the back was a long building from which poured cheering voices and TV football commentary. The bartender that emerged at Babasegun's shout was a pudgy, sweating man. He frowned at us in greeting, acknowledged Babasegun's order with a grunt. He brought the beers and glasses but forgot the bottle opener. It took him twenty minutes to return with that, by which time we had discovered that the glasses were crusted with dried beer foam. Babasegun spoke roughly to him about his bad service. He picked up the glasses and stomped away.

"The idiot is watching football," Babasegun said. "It's Man United and Chelsea today. That's why everyone's inside, that's why he's behaving like that."

"Sorry, not a big fan of football," I said.

"Me too—can't stand it. If I had remembered the match was today we would have gone to a bar that has no TV."

"It's okay here," I said. "As long as he brings us clean glasses."

"The problem is, he won't return for the next hour. Do you mind drinking from the bottle? Or should I go and get the glasses?"

His car key and mobile phone were on the table. "Watch these for me, some of the people who come here are thieves." Then he left.

Beside the front steps of the pavilion a suya mallam stood over a basin of blazing coals. Smoke swirled about his face, rose from the roasting meat, a cloud of aroma. I called him over and ordered some suya. "With plenty of onions and pepper," I said as he walked away. I watched him baste the skewered meat with groundnut oil, then place it on the wire grille. Oil dripped from the meat, coals burst into flame. After a few minutes he removed the meat from the grille and sliced it up, flapping his fingers now and again. He sprinkled the meat with ginger-and-chili powder, garnished it with sliced onions and diced tomato, then packed it in newspaper. He approached the table and placed the wrap before me, then strode away, counting my money.

Babasegun's phone rang.

The first two times, I sat back and enjoyed the music. The third time I reached over, picked it up, looked at the screen. The caller was "JK."

Babasegun arrived with the glasses as the phone rang for the seventh time. He frowned at the screen. He filled his glass to the

brim with beer and took a long drink, smacked his lips and licked
foam off them, then poured a refill.

"Who's JK?" I asked.

He froze with his hand around the Trophy bottle and stared at
me, face searching for an expression. Releasing his grip, he raised
the hand to rub his mouth. Then his gaze moved past my face,
over my shoulder, into the distance, from where his voice came.

"Joke," he said. "Her name is Joke."

∽

She was persistent, this Joke. Every time she called, he cut the
phone off. He talked about his wife, who was a small-goods
trader; about his three sons, who were his world entire; about
his university days, when he had high hopes he would one day
hold a better job than what he was now stuck with. The phone
kept ringing: his monologue was interrupted by short bursts of
Tupac's rap. One line, repeated over and over. *Somebody wake me
I'm dreaming.*

I was preparing to complain when he rose, snatched the phone
off the table and said, "A moment, please," in a fierce, breathless
voice, then marched off.

He strolled back nearly a quarter of an hour later. I said: "I finished the suya. It's best while it's hot. I couldn't just sit here and let
a good thing go to waste."

He stopped in front of his chair, gazed at me, then squeezed
closed one eyelid and pushed out his lips in a pout. "Okay. But I'll
get you back!" He bent down and grasped his kneecaps, then fell
back into the chair with a groan. He stretched his legs under the
table and his foot struck mine.

"What's going on between you and Joke?"

His neck stiffened. "None of your business!"

I shrugged, looked away, raised my glass and sipped.

"I don't like talking about it," he said.

Staring at the tabletop, I ran my fuck-you finger around the rim of my glass.

"She's my student," he said with a sigh. "We've been seeing each other for two years now, but I'm trying to end it. She doesn't want to stop."

"Your student! Interesting. What class is she in?"

"Senior Secondary Two."

"How old?"

"Sixteen."

"You lucky dog!"

A smile softened his face. "She's a bad girl, don't let her age fool you," he said.

"So why do you want to end it?"

He parted his lips to speak, but at that moment a wild cheer burst from the barroom, drowning out everything. Manchester United had scored.

When the celebration ended, I repeated my question. *"Because,"* Babasegun said, drawing out the word. He breathed in, breathed out, slow and steady. "She will soon put me in trouble. She's fucking everybody, small boys, big men, even some of my friends. The way she's going, she will soon catch something. She has aborted two times already. If she gets pregnant again, how will I know it's mine?"

"That bad?"

"Yes, she is. Rotten." Then he added quickly: "She was already that way before."

My curiosity was piqued by this spoiled young thing hidden away in a dead-end town. I wondered what she looked like, wondered how wild she really was. I wanted to know her.

"Let me help you," I said, and smiled at Babasegun, my cheeks aching with stiffness. "Let me take her off your hands. Let me make her forget you. Introduce me."

Babasegun threw back his head and laughed. His cheekbones

swayed, his tribal marks shifted, his foot knocked my shin under the table. He poured beer and drank, wiped his mouth with the back of his hand. "Bad boy!" he said, slapping the tabletop, rattling the bottles. "I knew you liked women, I knew you were my kind of guy. *My man!*" He stretched out his arm and we bumped fists. Then he turned serious, said:

"If I introduce you, forget it. She'll never do anything with you. She'll think I sent you to trap her. The only way you'll get her is on your own. But I can help."

ॐ

He gave me her mobile phone number and told me the best way to approach her. Be upfront about what you want, he said. Don't woo. Tell her to come and see you at your hotel.

That night, when he dropped me off at the hotel gate, I leaned into the passenger-side window and thanked him for being a good friend, one willing to share his beer and his girl. Then I asked the question.

"Are you sure you're through with her? You're sure you won't go back?"

"I'm sure," he said. "I'll never go back."

ॐ

The following day, after my class, about three o' clock, I called her.

"Hello? Who's this?"

"My name is Iggy. Is this Joke?"

"Yes."

"Hello, Joke."

"What do you want?"

She sounded different than I'd imagined. Colder, bolder. My heartbeat quickened. Her voice was attractive, husky and refined. Not your average small-town girl's.

"Actually, erm, I'm new in this town." I coughed to clear my throat. "I got your number from a friend who met you when he passed through here some months ago. He said you're a nice person to hang out with."

The phone line crackled, sounding like Babasegun's car player when the tape ran out.

"Joke? Are you there?"

"What's your friend's name?"

The fierceness in her voice caught me off guard. I said the first name that came to mind.

"Chinua. His name is Chinua."

Bush-fire static. I could feel the gears clicking in her head.

"I can't remember any Chinua from out of town," she said. Her voice softened, took on a faraway quality. "Chinua, Chinua . . . no, I don't think I've met any Chinua who doesn't live here. Are you sure that's who gave you my number?"

I released a long hiss of breath into the phone. "I got your number from a friend, and his name is Chinua, that's all. Can you come and meet me?" I said the name of my hotel and my room number. "There's something important I want to discuss with you."

"What is it?"

"Not on the phone."

"All right, when do you want me to come?"

I tried to speak but my throat was dry. I held the phone away from my mouth and coughed till I tasted rawness. I dabbed at my eyes with my knuckles, then raised the phone and said, "Come now."

"Today?"

"Yes. I'm waiting for you."

"Well, I'm not far from your hotel," she said. Short pause. "Give me an hour."

I was standing in the bathroom doorway when the phone line went dead. I walked to the bed, sat at the edge. One hour. Joke. Babasegun was right. He was a stand-up guy, he had delivered. A song rose in my head. *Somebody wake me I'm dreaming.*

The TV showed NN24. I pointed the remote control, changed the channel to MTV, and then raised the volume until the walls vibrated with music. On the screen, Lady Gaga in an Andy Warhol fantasy. Sterile. I glanced around: the room was a mess. I rose, swept everything off the bed—my dirty clothes, the pile of porn DVDs I watched at night on my laptop, the two books I'd brought along but hadn't yet begun reading, the TV remote control, and my skin lotion—and arranged the sheets.

ॐ

The next evening, Babasegun called my phone to give directions to a new bar, where we agreed to meet at seven. This was the third time he had phoned me, and I could tell he was more comfortable spending money on beer than on phone credits. He had so far refused to let me pay for my drinks; he always picked up the tab. On the phone he spoke in a rush, his greeting curt and his sentences short. Rude. He dropped the call while I was still speaking.

I left my room at a few minutes to seven and flagged down a motorcycle taxi in front of the hotel gate. I arrived at the rendezvous four minutes late. The Saab was parked by the roadside. The bar was outside. It was smaller, seedier, and more exposed than the bar opposite my hotel. Babasegun sat on a long wooden bench, which he shared with two men. He smiled when he saw me. He wore a tailor-made shirt in green and yellow nsibidi print. There was an opened bottle of Trophy on a stool in front of him. An empty bottle lolled at his feet.

"I don't like this place," I said as I settled beside him on the grime-patinaed bench. "Let's stick to the bar near my hotel. I'm sorry, I know you want to show me around, but I really need to settle that Wunmi business."

Babasegun looked at me with surprise. "What about Joke? I thought you met her yesterday?"

"No. She didn't come, she stood me up."

"Are you serious?"

"Of course I'm serious."

Babasegun drank from his glass, wiped his mouth back-handed. "That's strange, very strange," he said under his breath. His hand palmed his scarred cheek in slow circles. "You sure she didn't find out that you know me?"

"I don't know. If she did, it's not from me. I called her, we spoke, and we agreed to meet. She did not show up. I've been calling her since last night to find out what happened, but she's not answering—"

I stopped and listened; the hairs at the back of my neck prick-led. I turned around to find an old woman standing close, watch-ing me. Her eyelids were black with kohl. Her cotton-white hair was cornrowed. Her stringy arms, which rested akimbo on her hips, were covered with crude tattoos of names, dates, the birth details of her brood. Under the smell of mothballed fabric she gave off, I caught a whiff of catfish guts.

"Yes?" Babasegun said.

I waited for her to speak, then realized he was waiting for me.

"Yes what?" I asked, and, in a whisper: "Why is she staring at me?"

"Iya owns this bar. Tell her what you want to drink."

I avoided her red, tired eyes. "Trophy," I said. She made no move to leave.

"Iya's catfish peppersoup is the best in town," Babasegun said.

I nodded. He addressed her in Yoruba. She walked away.

Babasegun drank from his glass and then balanced it on his knee. "Now tell me what you told Joke," he said.

As I prepared to speak, his phone rang.

"Speak of the devil."

"Her?"

"Yes."

"Will you answer?"

"No."

I held out my hand. "Give it to me, let me speak to her."

He hesitated. The phone stopped ringing. I waited, my hand outstretched. The phone rang again. He handed it over.

"Hello, Joke," I said.

"Why are you doing this to me?" she yelled in my ear. "Tell me what I did!"

"This is not Babasegun. It's me, Iggy."

"What?"

"I called you yesterday, remember, the hotel? You were supposed to meet me."

"Why are you with Baba's phone?"

"He gave it to me to answer. He doesn't want to talk to you."

I could hear her breath whistling. On the horizon, far up in the starless sky, lightning sparked. The air was still, so clean it stung my throat. Babasegun watched me.

"Help me ask Baba what I did to him." Her tone had softened.

"No, I can't," I said in a harsh tone. I felt the urge to hurt her, to poke her in broken places. "But I can tell you why he doesn't want you anymore."

The expression of alarm on Babasegun's face made me feel better; I clamped my hand over my mouth to stifle my laughter. He threw me a weak, gloomy smile.

"Why?" Joke asked.

I could say it was because she fucked around; that he was afraid she would give him a baby or a disease; that he was tired of her—and all of those reasons would be true. But she was half woman, half child, and infatuated. For Babasegun's sake I had to let her down easy.

"Look, Joke, you're his student. He shouldn't have done anything with you. He wants to stop it now, before it's too late."

She laughed: a mirthless bark. "That's not the reason. Ask him to tell you the real reason."

"Okay, I'll ask him."

"I mean *now*. Ask him now. I'll wait."

I lowered the phone, turned to Babasegun, and rolled my eyes. "Joke says you should tell me the real reason you want to break up with her."

He arched his eyebrows into question marks. "The real reason?" he said in a loud voice. "She's been talking too much, she's been telling her friends about us, and now my wife has heard. The other teachers are becoming suspicious. If they find out, I'll be in trouble. There are other reasons I won't mention—no need to open our nyash in public. She knows we have to stop. She's just being stubborn."

I heard the angry buzz of her voice as I raised the phone. "*—big fat lies!*" she screamed into my ear.

"What he said seems reasonable, Joke." I held the phone away from my ear, looked around to make sure we were alone—the two men who shared the bench with us had left—and put the phone on loudspeaker. Her voice leaped out, rat-tat-tating.

"Don't believe him! He said I'm telling people about us, that his wife found out because of me? Am I the only girl he's friending in that school? I know like five girls, one of them is even my classmate! How come his wife didn't hear about them? Then he's talking about teachers—that he will get in trouble. Let him not make me laugh! Which of the male teachers are not doing what he's doing? Which of them don't have girlfriends?"

I set the phone on the bench between me and Babasegun. He stood up. "I'm coming," he whispered, and hurried away like a man with a full bladder. Ha ha, I thought.

"What? What is he saying?" Joke asked.

"Nothing." I drummed the bench with my fingers, and then said quickly, before she started up again: "Now, Joke, calm down, I've heard you. But all the things you've said don't change the fact that Babasegun doesn't want to be with you anymore."

"Listen well, brother," she said, her voice unsteady, "when he was chasing me two years ago, I refused, I didn't want to do anything with him, but he didn't stop, he worried me until I agreed. Now that he has got what he wanted he wants to throw me away just like that? No way, never! We will continue what we're doing."

There was a movement behind me. Babasegun approached with Iya, who bore a tray from which rose wreaths of steam. I picked up the phone, turned off the loudspeaker, held it to my ear.

"I don't know what to say," I said. "I can only advise you. You can't force a man when he says he's had enough."

"I said listen to me! I know Baba well, he doesn't want to stop, he just wants me to beg!"

The bench creaked as Babasegun sat down. Iya placed a Trophy beer, a glass, and a chinaware bowl in front of me. A big-headed, black-skinned catfish bobbed in the broth that filled the bowl to brimming. I looked away when Joke spoke.

"I know what I'm saying. This is not the first time he's told me it's over. If he really wants to stop, how come he calls me every time he needs me? When I call him he won't pick up his phone, but whenever he wants me to do something he will start calling me! He's been doing this for more than a month, since September, telling me it's over, refusing to answer my calls. But last Sunday he called me in the morning, he picked me up from my house, we did it in the backseat of his car before he dropped me at church. If you don't believe me, ask him!"

A wave of exhaustion washed over me. This conversation would go on forever if I allowed it. It was now clear there was no hope for me here.

"I believe you," I said.

All I wanted at this moment was to dig my teeth into catfish flesh, to eat my peppersoup and drink my beer. As if she read my thoughts, Joke said: "You answered his phone so you deliver this message to him. I have gone out with men who are not ashamed to be with me, so I don't need him, that common schoolteacher, with his ugly tribal marks! I have never asked him for money, never collected one kobo from him! Ask him. Even the times he made me pregnant, I removed it with my own money. I don't need him!"

"Okay, I agree, you don't need him. Can I tell him you will never contact him again?"

The phone burned against my cheek, overheated from talking. The air smelled like rain. Babasegun was eating my peppersoup.

"Joke?"

"*I can't!*" she wailed. So loudly that I winced and jerked my head away. Then I returned the phone to my ear.

"Why can't you?"

"I don't know, I don't understand." Her voice was choked. "Every time I see Baba my feelings get stronger. When I'm not with him I'm always thinking about him. Anytime we quarrel, anytime he refuses to answer my call, I become useless. Because of him I can't stay with one boyfriend. None of them can be like him. It's like something is tying us together. Baba knows what it is. He knows what he has done to me. Let him release me. I will go, I will stop begging, I will stop calling his phone, but let him release me first."

I looked at Babasegun eating my peppersoup, and wondered about him. Whatever he had done to her, he had done it well.

"I'll talk to Babasegun," I said, and glanced again at him. He was ripping off catfish chunks with his teeth and fingers. He shook his head in warning, his jaws munching. "I have to go now. But don't worry, I'll tell him what you said."

"Thank you," she said. "Can I call you later? To get Baba's reply?"

"No. I'll call you. Bye."

I held out the phone to Babasegun. He grasped it with the thumb and pinkie of his left hand, and dropped it in his lap. He licked his fingers, one after the other, sucking the nails. A pile of bones lay beside the peppersoup bowl. He followed my gaze.

"You have to eat it while it's hot," he said with a tomcat grin. "I couldn't just sit here and watch you waste a good thing!"

∂⊃

It started to rain on the drive to the hotel. A few fat drops at first, which struck the earth like bird shit. Then churning wind, dust spraying the windshield, sand gritting in my eyes and between my teeth. The water came in hard, a pounding roar. We had wound up the windows; the glass was misted over. Few cars appeared out of the muffled night. Raindrops glinted in the truncated beam of the Saab headlights. Babasegun was hunched forward, his nose almost touching the steering wheel, his hands latched tight around it. I hoped he could see where he was going, because I couldn't.

I looked up when I heard him curse, but it was too late, the pothole was right in front of us, a rite of passage. The front of the car dipped, the underside scraped the road, and the tires spun, throwing up waves of muddy water. Babasegun yanked the gearstick and throttled the car. The engine whined, the car bucked like a rodeo bull, and then clambered out of the pothole. Moments after my shout of joy, the engine coughed, shed horsepower, stalled, and then fired up again. The chassis lurched forward. The engine grumbled and hissed and spewed angry white steam clouds. Then the car rolled to a stop, raindrops drumming the roof.

"Kai!" Babasegun exclaimed, and smacked the steering wheel with the flat of his hand. He turned the key, rattled it—nothing.

"We're in the middle of the road." I turned my head to see if headlights were approaching.

Babasegun muttered under his breath. He set the gearstick in neutral, threw open the door and stepped out, wedged his shoulder against the doorframe and strained forward, guiding the steering wheel with his right hand. I remained seated. If he didn't ask, I wouldn't offer.

By the time he slid into the driver's seat and pulled the door
shut, he was drenched. Water rolled down his face and neck, his
arms, dripping onto the seat, pattering the rubber floor mat. He
turned to me and said, "We'll have to leave the car here. We won't
find okadas at this time, not in the rain. We'll have to walk to the
taxi park behind Town Hall. It's not far."

He gave the car a quick onceover, then placed his hand on the
door handle. "Ready?"

"For what?"

"To go, it's getting late." He drew his mobile phone from his
right hip pocket and looked at the screen. "It's past eleven."

I folded my arms across my chest. "There's no way I'm going
out in that rain."

"Ah!" Babasegun sank back into his seat, raised his hand and
rubbed his cheek. "This kind of rain doesn't stop for hours—we'll
be here all night if we wait." I remained silent. "Please," he said.
"I've already stayed out too late. My wife traveled yesterday. My
boys are alone at home."

"I can't go out in that rain. You can leave me. I'll lock up and
return your key tomorrow."

"I can't do that, I can't leave you here," Babasegun said in a sullen voice. He rested his forehead against the side glass. "This rain
won't stop today. Look, it's getting heavier."

It was. The car was hemmed in by walls of water.

"Is that your final decision? That we should wait out the rain?"

"I have to. I'm sorry."

"Okay, I give up." He reached for his phone and punched in
a number, then held it to his ear. "Answer, answer," he muttered
under his breath, tapping the steering wheel with his free hand.
"Hello?" he said in a relieved voice. "Joke?"

I stared at him in amazement.

"I have a problem. My car broke down and I'm stuck in this
storm. Long story, I'll tell you later. The children are alone at home.

Mama Wasiu traveled. Can you go to my house right now? The key is where I usually leave it, under the big flowerpot."

He listened. I strained to hear.

"Send them to bed. You sleep in my room," he said. "I'll see you in the morning. Don't forget to take along your school uniform so I can drop you off. Your toothbrush is in my toilet bag. Okay, bye."

He tossed the phone on the dashboard, and stared out through the windshield, silent. I too remained silent, thinking. Then I cleared my throat.

"Tomorrow's the last day of my workshop," I said. "The club is organizing a farewell party at the bar opposite my hotel. Starts at five."

"When are you leaving?" he asked.

"Early the following day—car's already booked. It will pick me from the hotel at eight."

He was silent a moment. "At least we can agree on one thing."

"What's that?"

"You like Trophy."

"I do! I'm a fan now."

He laughed. Lightning flashed. I caught a glint in his eyes. And then his profile, black in the dark.

He asked, "What about Wunmi? Do you still want her?"

"Yes. I meant to ask your advice about that."

"Okay then, listen up . . ."

ᛒ

His plan worked. Wunmi was everything I wanted—especially with the knowledge that the first time was the last. My only regret was that I couldn't chat about it afterwards with Babasegun over a cold bottle of Trophy, or over the phone.

Babasegun did not attend my farewell party and he did not pick up my calls. The last time I spoke with him was in that car, the black vinyl-upholstered Saab that in my mind was linked forever with Tupac's music. Two men in a dead car in a rainstorm in a sleeping town, chatting long into the night, until we grew drowsy from the sound of our voices, until I climbed into the backseat and curled up in sleep, and woke up the next morning to find a bright new sun staring at me through the rain-washed windshield, and Babasegun gone.

The Little Girl with Budding Breasts and a Bubblegum Laugh

He began to love her when she was nine and had breasts the size of tangerines. She was still in her impetuous phase—she dashed about the house in her underclothes and shrieked with laughter. He was her cousin, her big brother; he was fifteen years older than her. Nobody saw anything suspicious when he clasped her under the arms and spun her—squealing and kicking—in a maypole circle, then pressed her to his chest, all the while grinning like a Nok mask to hide the consternation that her milk-and-sugar smell, her puppy warmth, awakened in his belly. When she was eleven and he came to visit because his uncle, her father, was lying on the sickbed, he placed her on his knee and stroked her legs till she roped her arms round his neck and suffocated him in a cloud of peppermint sniffles and talcum sweat. That night, while he fondled himself, her father died.

The week she turned fourteen she came to live with his family. By this time her mother had remarried and they now called her a problem child. It was true: she was no longer the happy person he had known. She had secrets and acne eruptions, mood swings and no-sugar days. When his female friends visited she fell into bottomless silences, she darted furious glances at him, but when he tried to pacify her by reviving their games from the past, she told him, every time, *fuck off*. She wore makeup, she dressed like a woman. She locked herself in the bathroom and wouldn't emerge until the whole house was bathed in the dead-flower scent of cheap cosmetics. Her mobile phone was her constant companion and confidante: she would curl up in her favorite corner of the sofa and murmur into it for hours; or sit hunched over the screen and with wild boneless fingers tip-tap the number codes to some life-or-death game; or plug in her earphones and—swinging, bobbing, wiggling her head—mouth the lyrics of "Whenever, Wherever" as she sleepwalked through chores. She hated rules, restrictions, convention. His mother was always complaining of her insolence, always warning her against the dangers of the street, against friends who had no home training.

Her quirks of temper had become so habitual that when she announced to the family at dinner one day that she had changed her name, nobody said a word. After his younger brother gathered the plates and went into the kitchen to wash up, his mother ahemed to declare the battle open, and looked at his father.

So what do we call you now, madam? his father asked.

My name is Shakira.

The twins—his sixteen-year-old sisters, who attended the same school as her and watched the same MTV videos and wore the same tight, bright, designer-label clothes—exchanged glances. His mother took a long drink of water. The glass clinked against her teeth.

I see, his father said. And your surname—is that still good enough for you?

She fiddled with her phone. From the kitchen came the clatter of plates and the hiss of running water. It was the only sound in the house.

His mother erupted. Answer when you're spoken to!

She pushed her chair back from the table and stood up. Yes, she said, looking down at his father, ignoring his mother.

Yes what? his mother said.

My father's name will *always* be good enough for me. The way she inflected the words, the way she locked eyes with his mother, the expression on her face, made his mother lean forward and grip the edges of the table. Then she turned her back on her aunt, on her three cousins all older than her, on his father who had agreed to take her in when her mother could no longer put up with her, and stalked out.

His father turned to the woman shaking with fury by his side and placed his hand over hers. Ignore her, he said, it's just adolescence, she will outgrow it.

They followed his father's advice: they acted as if nothing had happened. But she stuck to her position; she feigned deafness whenever her christened name was called. So they ignored her.

Despite the forbidding of any mention of her adopted name, they found that, with time, they had begun, at first in ignorance, then later with mounting certainty, to blame her rudenesses on her alter ego. The longer she insisted that she was this impostor, this Shakira, the more, in their minds, she became her.

He—who saw her as she would always be: not this teenager with telephonic secrets and trivial obsessions, but the little girl with budding breasts and a bubblegum laugh—called her Shakira. His mother disagreed. His father and sisters, at the behest of his mother, implored him to abandon his opposite stance. He refused.

჻

On the evening of the following Friday he returned from his workplace, the regional headquarters of a global brand management firm, with a batch of tickets to an all-night hip-hop concert, and called his cousin and sisters to come and collect the gifts. His mother waited till the girls had run screaming with excitement out of the sitting room, and then broached the topic.

You know we're not calling her by that name. Don't support her in this nonsense.

But I have to call her something, he said.

Call her by her name!

She won't answer me.

Then let her be nameless.

Isn't this too much trouble over a nickname?

Look. I know she has always been your favorite cousin and you will support her in everything, but in this matter, listen to me.

But I have to call her something, he said.

Okay. I've said my own.

He trod upstairs, shed his clothes in his bedroom, and went into the bathroom. He was in the bathtub when he remembered he had not informed the girls he would attend the concert with them. He called out his sisters' names, but none of them responded. He had soap in his eyes; the talk with his mother had upset him. So he yelled *Shakira!* again and again in a voice that rattled the loose lid of the toilet cistern. When she rapped on the bathroom door, he told her to wait downstairs for him when she was ready, and to pass on the message to his sisters.

She was ready, waiting for him, but his sisters were not. They were not going, his mother told him, and neither would "that girl" if she knew what was good for her. Okay, he said, his sisters had made their choice—very well, their loss—but he and Shakira would go. His mother struck back: she demanded the keys to her car, the 2002 Toyota Camry that he had driven and serviced with his money since he started working seven months ago. He tossed the keys on the table, and signaling to his silent, expressionless, jeans and T-shirt dressed cousin to follow, he walked out.

He did not enjoy the concert. He did not expect to. But she did. She pushed through the screaming crowd till she reached the front of the stage, and she snapped innumerable photos with her phone camera, and sent them as messages to his sisters. She danced and sang along until her clothes were soaked with sweat and her voice became a croak. She pestered him for money to buy sweetened alcohol, and sometime in the early hours of the morning, when the concert was winding down, she leapt onstage to plaster his change—note after note, and she shrieked with joy as she did it—on the sweat-slick forehead of her music idol.

By four in the morning she was dull-eyed with fatigue. It was too late to head for home, too early to return to the fight that was waiting for them, he told her. To pass the time he led her by hand on a stroll of the concert grounds, till, in desperation, she suggested a hotel. *Anywhere I can sleep, please,* she begged, and stamped her feet, tugged at his arm, pressed her cold face into his neck. He laughed, to show her he wasn't eager. She overpowered him with a hug.

They found a small hotel two streets away from the concert venue. By the time he finished filling the check-in form she had fallen asleep against his back. *My sister—attended the concert— home is far,* he explained to the receptionist, who yawned and fisted her eyes as she handed him the key and a roll of tissue paper. He carried her up three flights of stairs, her head dangling over one arm and her legs over the other. When he arrived at the room that bore their number he tried to set her down to unlock the door, but she whined her displeasure and clung to his shoulders.

The door creaked open, then swung shut, and the darkness of the room wrapped itself around him with a smell of dust and poultry disinfectant. He felt along the wall for the light switch and snapped it on. Yellow mist flooded his vision. There was a movement—he caught sight of the tall, unshaven, wild-eyed man staring at him from across the room, a lifeless child clutched in his arms like a sack of something stolen. After the shock of recognition he found the courage to laugh at the man in the mirror, who was not him, would never be him.

He looked down at her, this weight in his arms. He walked to the bed and placed her on it. She whimpered, drew up her knees, and crossed her arms over her chest. He slipped off her sandals, pulled the blanket up to her neck, then turned on the air conditioner, switched off the light, and lay down on the carpet at the foot of the bed.

He couldn't sleep. His imagination grew insect legs and crawled all over his nerves. He scratched his arms, rubbed his face, slapped at his feet. When the bug bites became unbearable on one side, he rolled over.

He was alerted by the rustle of bedclothes, and the bed creaked as she sat up.

What is it?

Nothing, he said. Go back to sleep.

You don't have to sleep on the floor, there's enough space here, she said, patting the bed.

He gritted his teeth. His fingers dug into the rug.

You heard me?

I hear you, he said.

He waited until she settled back, then he rose. A chink in the drapes let in a sliver of streetlight, which sliced across the bed. She was curled up on her side, and her head rested on her hands, which were clasped together. He walked to the empty side of the bed and crawled under the blanket, into her fragrance.

At first he lay still. Then he turned to face her back, to assume her fetal position. His movement rocked the bed, and she shifted her weight. She moved again, and again, heat rising in the closing gap between their bodies. She had slid across half of the bed; the blanket was bunched about their legs; breakaway tendrils of her plaited hair tickled his face. He saw the trembling in the back of her neck and heard the hum, the thump, the irregular motoring of her heart. He inched forward his hand and touched her shoulder, and she heaved a monsoon sigh, rolled over to face him, and wound her arms round his neck.

∽

He awoke the way one does on the eve of a long journey. It was daybreak. A spray of sunlight dappled his right shoulder, and his cousin—warm-fleshed, fully clothed—lay in his arms. His groin was pressed against her haunches. He disentangled his arms, stretched them wide, and yawned. Then he sat up and said, Good morning.

She rolled over to look at him. The smile on her sleep-puffed

face, the affectionateness, the unaffectedness of the smile, made him
want to lean down and bruise her mouth with kisses.

Morning, she said, her words muffled by a wide pink yawn.
Her teeth glistened like wet pebbles. Her breath, that old familiar,
wafted into his face. He fought it ferociously, the urge that knifed
through him, but he was overpowered, and he lowered his head.

After the kiss they avoided each other's eyes and rose to prepare
for whatever lay ahead. While she used the bathroom, he fixed
the bed. She emerged from the crash of flushing water to find him
blocking her path.

He said her name: his voice trembled. I'm sorry, I took
advantage . . .

She shushed him with a snigger. Don't be silly, nothing happened.
And I've told you, but you won't hear—my name is Shakira!

&

They had breakfast at the hotel, and then headed home. When
they entered the gate of the house they met the twins digging up
weeds in the garden, and she skipped from his side to join them.
He walked on, followed by the trill of her voice, till he reached the
front door and went in. The falsetto of his father's singing floated
from the sitting room, above the burr of the vacuum cleaner. His
mother stood midway up the staircase, polishing the mahogany
banister. In response to his greeting she threw him a baleful
glance, then turned away to instruct his younger brother to water
the potted dieffenbachia that stood beside the hallway bookshelf.

For the rest of Saturday he kept to his room.

&

The next day, Sunday, he woke up late, to a silent house. Everyone
had left for church. He went downstairs to find something to
eat. The kitchen was untidy—they had left in a hurry. The floor
around the dustbin was strewn with yam peels and onion skins

and Maggi wrappers. A used pot sat on the cooker, and the serving ladle rested in a pool of amber-colored oil on the countertop, beside the uncapped, sweating bottle of cranberry juice. The sink was stacked with plates.

He'd opened the sink tap and squirted dishwashing liquid into the collected water, when he realized there were only five plates. He screwed the tap closed and dried his hands on the seat of his pajamas, then ran from the kitchen, up the stairs, to the door of the girls' bedroom.

At the first knock, she answered. He entered to find her sitting cross-legged on the bed, playing a game on her phone. She was still in her nightdress, the yellow, Daffy Duck–patterned one. The hemline rode up her thighs, revealing the slopes of her knees.

Hey, he said, as he shut the door and leaned against it.

Morning, she said, not looking up. Her fingers skittered across the keypad, scoring points.

Can I sit?

She shrugged in reply, and he walked to the bed, sank down beside her, and asked: Why didn't you go to church with them? No answer. Her breath quickened.

Are you not talking to me? he asked, and reached his hand forward to grip her ankle.

Her fingers stopped moving; the phone drooped in her hands; the game played the same cartoon melody over and over.

Looking at her averted face, he remembered how, when she was little, every time he went to her parents' house he used to place her in his lap, and while she swung her legs about and sucked the sweets he'd brought her, he chatted over her head as he stroked her knees. He felt a stab of nostalgia for those happy, guiltless days. He wanted to show her that she was still his favorite, that the years hadn't eroded his affection, that the previous night hadn't changed anything, so he lifted her leg, pulled it toward him, placed her ankle in his lap, and caressed her knee. His hand whispered over her skin.

You're beautiful, you know that?

At his words, she looked up, and a cloud-shadow of expressions flitted across her face; then she rested her head against his shoulder. He eased her sideways, onto the bed, pinned her down with his chest, worked his knee between her legs. When she gasped, he kissed her.

&

You're sure you love me?

She lay on her belly beside him, with her chin propped on his chest. Her right leg was cocked at the knee, the foot waving in the air.

Yes, he said. His hand played round-and-round-the-garden with her pants line, and when his fingers took two steps and tickled, she squirmed and clamped her thighs.

Why do you love me? she asked, staring at his beard stubble, at his lips, into his eyes.

Because, he said, with a jerk of his shoulders. I've loved you for a long time, since you were nine.

Serious? I didn't know. Her eyes shone. Her breath scalded his face.

After a pause. So what do you love about me? she asked.

Everything, he said, and nuzzled her cheek. His nose left a dab of sweat on her skin. His right hand, in slow circles, rubbed the back of her thighs.

Like?

Like, you know . . .

My ass?

Come on, don't say that.

Then tell me, what do you like?

Okay, he said, and dug his elbow into the bed, braced his jaw against his fisted hand, stared at her with widened eyes and pouted lips, a playful face that fell away as he continued—since you're forcing me. I like your eyes. I like the way they light up when you're happy. I like your legs. I like the way you walk, especially when you're hurrying, the way you throw your feet, like a child who's about to fall. I like your nose, and your mouth, and your breath. I like the way your breath smells. Like melted ice cream.

Wow, she said in a hushed, wondering voice; and then she adjusted her legs. His hand slid between her thighs.

But.

But what? he asked, and kissed her earlobe.

But won't it cause trouble, that we're, you know, cousins?

Yes. It will.

So what will we do?

We have to keep it a secret, at least for now. People won't understand my feelings for you. They'll say you're too young, that . . . that we're related. We can't let anyone know.

Okay.

That's my girl, he said, and flashed a broad, toothy smile. Then he dipped his head, and chased her elusive lips with a teasing *zzz-ing* in the back of his throat.

At the sound of his father's car pulling into the driveway their lips broke apart. He scrambled to his feet, adjusted the crotch of his pajama bottoms. I'll see you later, he said over his shoulder, walking with short, awkward, frantic steps toward the door.

ᕼᴓ

After lunch was over and he'd withdrawn to his bedroom, the summons that he had ceased to expect was announced. His brother delivered the message with a serious expression fixed on his happy child's face, and then he added:

Mama is *very* angry with you.

He entered the sitting room to find his mother and father waiting for him. He drew up beside their seats and thrust his hands into his trouser pockets, to hide their trembling.

Your mother is very angry with you—and so am I, his father said. Then he waved to the opposite chair: Take the weight off your feet.

With a quick glance at his mother, he sat down, and fixed his gaze on his father.

His father said, Your mother and I have been discussing your cousin's behavior, and to tell you the truth, we're tired of it. But your conduct is also giving us cause for concern. Why won't you listen when we tell you not to call her that—he turned to his wife—what is she, darling, a singer?—and turned back to his son—*that* Colombian singer's name? Not allowing time for a reply, he continued: The only good thing to come out of that country is Garcia Marquez. By the way, have you read his latest—

Papa, stick to the topic, his mother interposed.

Sorry, dear. He frowned at his son. We already have enough trouble from that young lady—we don't need any more from you. So don't call her by that name again, okay?

But Papa, it's just a nickname!

His father exchanged looks with his wife, licked his lips, cleared his throat, and lowered his voice. It's a bit more serious than that.

How?

His mother took charge of the silence. Look here, she said, in a voice that shook with contained anger, since you're now too big to abide by the rules we set in this house, maybe it's time you moved out. You have a job and you have savings, you can afford to pay rent. Go and be lord and master in your own house.

At his mother's words, he knew it was over, the fight was lost. To hell with the stupid name, he thought. He would do what he had to do to remain where he had to be.

He arranged his face into a mask of pleading. But, Mama, you know I'm saving up for my master's, he said in a subdued voice. I can't afford to take out of my savings to pay for an apartment. You know that.

Now we're getting somewhere, his mother said, and leaned forward in her chair. So open your ears and listen. As long as you're my son and you live under my roof, you must obey me. She smacked her palm against the armrest to emphasize her next words. From today, you have to stop calling her by that name.

He met her gaze, then dropped his eyes. I hear you, Mama, he said.

℘

That night, after dinner, he sent her a text message to meet him in the grove of plantain trees by the canal behind the house. She sent back an instant, one-letter reply. *K.*

He waited beside the tallest plantain tree, which was stooped with fruit. There was a strong breeze, and the big, fanlike leaves waved and rustled above his head and cast swooping shadows on the rough ground.

He'd begun to worry—then she appeared. She lit her path with the screen light of her mobile phone, and when he whispered her name, she increased her pace, scrunching dead leaves underfoot.

Shakira, *Shakira!* she said with a chiding tone as she drew up to him. She stuck her phone in the waistband of her denim miniskirt, and then stood before him with her arms akimbo and her weight resting on one hip.

He reached out to hold her waist, then drew her forward. She resisted his pull, twisting from side to side and beating his shoulders lightly with her fists. His mouth bumped her nose, her cheek, her chin, before locking onto her lips. She moaned in protest; then opened her teeth and leaned against him.

When they drew apart, he said, That's what I called you about. I can't call you Shakira anymore.

Her shoulders stiffened. Why?

Mama spoke to me this afternoon. She warned me that if I call you Shakira again, I'll have to pack out. So I told her I wouldn't.

She snorted with anger. Okay, leave me alone, she said in a stinging voice, and dropped her hands to pry open his grip.

Don't be like that. Wait, *wait*—what do you want me to do? Her fingers dug into his skin, so he released her waist, and caught her wrist. If I disobey Mama, I'll have to leave. Then what will happen to us?

She turned her face aside and said in a flat voice: I don't know. I don't care.

Stop acting like a spoiled child, this is serious, he said. He placed his palm against her cheek and turned her face toward him with gentle pressure. Her eyes glittered with resentment. When he stroked the curve of her jaw, murmuring candyfloss words, a teardrop broke from her lashes and rolled down, wetting his hand.

Leave me alone, I want to go, she said.

Please.

I said leave me alone!

The shrillness of her cry startled him into letting go. She turned to leave, but he ran ahead of her and spread out his arms, blocking her path.

Stop it, Shakira. Okay, I give in. I'll call you the name.

She halted, raised her hand to flick away her tears, and beamed at him. He was wary of the flux of her moods, so he left his arms outspread, in case she tried to bolt. When she walked up and rested her forehead against his chest, he embraced her with force.

This is what we'll do . . .

He would call her Shakira, but only when they were alone; he would search for an apartment, so they could be alone together. She interrupted his words to say that she would run away if he left, that his parents were wasting their time if they thought they could control her by punishing him—and then, in a lower, unsteady voice, she said that she would follow him to his new house if he wanted. After she spoke, his arms dropped from her shoulders, he stepped back, and came up against a tree. Then he asked her if she meant it.

I do.

He spun round and slapped the tree in joy. He turned, lifted her off the ground and whirled her around, then pushed her against the tree, and kissed her laughing wet lips; then dropped to his knees, pressed his head against her skirt, and kissed her. When his face pushed under her skirt, her giggles caught in her throat. She stiffened, and begged him to stop, her hands pushing, pulling his head. He lurched to his feet and smeared her lips with the smell of herself, then drew back his head to ask her, his voice guttural, if he should. She said, *no please, no please,* but made no effort to break away, as his weight trapped her against the tree, his hands squeezed and prodded, and his lips covered her face with a snail trail of saliva. *Yes please,* he said in a whispery simoom voice, and tugged her hand downwards. At the touch of his flesh she opened her mouth in a soundless cry and fell against him; then burst into tears, her shoulders shaking.

He released her hand, took a step backward, and zippered his trousers. He watched in silence as she drew herself up, tried to walk away, stumbled and threw out her hand to steady herself, then turned round and hid her face against the tree. When her sobs abated to the occasional sniffle, he said, I'm sorry, I lost control, don't cry, nothing happened. He approached her, put his hand on her shoulder, then arranged her clothes. He stooped to pick her phone from where it had fallen, and handed it to her, then placed his hands on her hips, pressed his mouth against her hair, and said: Tell me the truth, are you a virgin?

She nodded. Her hair scrubbed his face.

ஐ

She didn't appear for breakfast or dinner, and she didn't take his phone calls or reply to his text messages for the three days that followed. The first day, Monday, at the dinner table, when his mother sent his brother to call her, she sent back word that she was ill. Tuesday was his brother's birthday, his eleventh, and after the candles were blown out, the wishes made, he sent the birthday boy to her room with a wedge of cake, a cold Coke, and a stapled note. He awoke on Wednesday morning to find the note slipped under his door, unopened. Wednesday evening, when he arrived from the office, he met his father in the upstairs hallway and asked him in a by-the-way tone if he had seen her.

Yes, funny you asked, his father replied, staring at him with a creased brow, she just ran past me with a bowl of cornflakes!

Can you imagine, she's angry at me because I refused to call her Shakira, he said, and then mustered all his willpower to sustain the grin with which he met his father's guffaws.

On Thursday, he rose early, got ready, and left. But when the gate clanged shut behind him, he reversed the car and parked by the fence of the house, to wait for her to emerge on her way to school. A quarter of an hour went by before she appeared, accompanied by his sisters. He called out to her but she refused to answer, and hurried away with the twins staring after her in amazement. He could dare nothing but stand and watch her go, his distress concealed behind a fractured smile.

I refused to call her Shakira, that's why she's angry with me, he told the twins, then throttled the car until it wailed with power and jumped forward with a spray of dust and stones.

That night at dinner, after his father commented on her absence, his sisters, their tones shrill with reproach, shared the story of their cousin's impoliteness toward their brother. His mother's glance of approval turned the rice bolus in his mouth to ash. He let his fork fall to his plate, and wiping his lips with the back of his hand, he rose from the table and mumbled, I had a long day at the office, I'm sorry, I need to rest. He shuffled away with heavy steps and climbed the stairs one at a time, his footfalls ringing through the house. When he reached the upstairs landing, he dashed soft-footed to the door of the girls' bedroom, but found it locked.

℘

On the night of Friday the sixteenth—a humid, starless night—he headed toward the house like a farm animal to the slaughter, his heartbeats frenetic from a conviction he couldn't shake off. He'd sent her a stream of text messages throughout the day, begging forgiveness, confessing regret, asking her to meet him. By the close of work he had received no reply, so he called her number, but her phone was switched off.

He was scuffing the soles of his loafers on the front doormat when he heard her voice. It came from the sitting room. He stopped and listened; crept forward and listened. His mother was now talking, her words indistinct.

He tiptoed to the sitting room doorway to hear better, and then peered in. She sat alone with his mother, the two figures side by side, his crime and punishment. Her face looked wan, subdued by distress; but it could have been the lighting, which was dull. She was staring at her feet, which never used to be still, but were now pressed together, toe to heel. Her hands were clasped between her knees, and she sat hunched over on the chair's edge.

. . . called you down is because I won't stand for any of this childishness anymore, his mother was saying in a low-pitched voice. Her head was cocked to one side. She fixed her niece in her stare. It's no longer about the name. It's about respect for your elders, about taking responsibility for your decisions. If you won't change your mind I'll have to send you back to your mother, because to tell you the truth, I've had enough.

Before she spoke, he knew her reply.

I'll go. Her voice rasped in her throat. She coughed, and then added: Tomorrow.

ߏ

Again, that night, she did not come down for dinner, and the conversation at the table was about her departure. His mother ate little; she buffeted the air with sighs and spoke in monosyllables. When his father glanced up from the book he was reading and said that maybe her going away was not such a bad thing, his mother hissed and shot furious looks with haphazard aim. Then she spoke in a slow, shaking voice about her dead twin brother, about his stubbornness, which his daughter had inherited.

I'll miss Shakira, said his brother, sweeping a glum, defiant look round the table.

I'll miss her too, his mother said, and smiled at her youngest child, her eyes glistening.

He finished his meal, bid good night, and retreated to his bedroom. It was past midnight before the upstairs hallway light went off. He swung his legs off the bed, waited in the dark for the sound of shutting doors to cease, then counted to five hundred before he stood up and slipped from the room, leaving the door ajar. He crossed to the staircase and sank to a crouch on the second step. He was hidden from anybody who emerged from the bedrooms, but if he leaned forward he could see the end of the hallway, where the bathroom was. He settled to wait.

Five times during his vigil the bathroom was used, but every time it was by someone else. A cock had crowed and a car blaring fuji music had sped past on the road, before she emerged. He waited for her to finish, he stood in front of the door until she flushed, then he turned the handle.

She whipped up her head and opened her mouth to complain, but when she saw him, she pressed a hand over her mouth and backed away. He pulled the door closed and turned the key. Placing his palms together, he held them in front of him, beseeched her as he advanced. Please, I beg you, just hear what I have to say.

No, she muttered, shaking her head side to side, don't.

She was backed up against the wall beside the toilet bowl. She held onto the cistern for support, but when the lid rattled from her trembling, she removed her hand. He drew up in front of her. His bare feet, as he rocked on his heels, made sucking noises on the wet floor tiles. He raised his arms to embrace her, but she flinched away, then turned her side to him, folded her arms across her chest, pressed her face against the wall, and squeezed her eyes shut.

He whispered into the ear that was turned to him, coaxing her with words that he had whetted over days. His hand rubbed her shaking shoulder, and then traveled down her arm, over her belly, across her hip. Beneath his fingers, her muscles quivered. His words fluttered strands of her hair and sent ripples through her cheek. Heat rose from her skin with a bruised scent. His hand moved again, growing bolder. He stroked her face. He smoothed her hair. He patted her belly, traced patterns around her navel. When his fingers slipped under her nightdress, she whimpered, opened her eyes, and dropped her arms.

Come, my love, he said to her, and led her by the hand out of the bathroom, across the hallway, into the night.

Godspeed and Perpetua

· 1 ·

On the day she turned seven months, three weeks, and six days old, the Anabraba child contracted an infection that by nightfall had turned her head the size of a watermelon. Her mother, unable to handle the thought of losing a piece of her soul to the dustbin of all things flesh, abandoned the fever-wracked infant with the father and fled to the Citadel of Fire and Miracles, a nearby church. The father was a thirty-five-year-old career civil servant and a first-time parent: he was not equipped, by training or experience, for the undertaking.

When the mother returned to the house after three days of fast and prayer, she found the child alive. A lifetime of change had taken place in the time she was away. Now it was only the sound of her husband's voice that had power to calm the baby's cries, to lull her to sleep. She ate with no trouble when it was her father's hand that fed her; she gurgled with delight when it was her father's hand that bathed her. The father had in the past shown no interest in these motherly duties, but now he volunteered for them, he even altered his work schedule to allow for them. His wife saw through the excuse of affection that he gave as his reason. He was the one who had stayed behind, he believed he had saved the child, so his plan, she was sure, was to take over the role of caregiver and keep for himself all of their daughter's love.

᠀

Godspeed Anabraba, in the ignorance of childhood, made a pledge to himself never to fail at anything. His father, a tall, handsome

man who was renowned as a singer and dancer, was a fisherman whose offspring were strewn across the ports of the Niger
Delta, so Godspeed had to fend for himself from a young age.
His mother—who remained unmarried after the mishap of unexpected pregnancy—did her best to ensure he attended primary
school, but he had to put himself through secondary school by the
work of his hands. Godspeed was a bright, dedicated student, and
by the end of his secondary education he had secured a scholarship
from the British colonial government to attend university in the
mother country.

On his return eleven years later to become a central member of his
young country's ruling bureaucracy, Godspeed, after erecting a man-
sion in his late mother's village, decided to take a wife. He set about
this task in a detached, punctilious manner: he considered only the
prettiest and most accomplished maidens from the best families. As
expected of a man who viewed failure as a sign of bad character, he
succeeded in his search. There was no exaggeration when the bulletin
board of the oldest church in the village carried the notice:

We publish the banns of marriage between Godspeed Anabraba
(senior civil servant and pride of our community)
and Perpetua Young-Harry (graduate of the Maryland School of
Catering and second daughter of Chief S. K. Young-Harry),
both of this Parish. If any of you know cause or just impediment why
these persons should not be joined together, ye are to declare it . . .

Even defeated suitors of the bride-to-be, astonished by this an-
nouncement, agreed it was a match that for convenience couldn't
be faulted.

But the union had more faults than the tectonic plates of
Nippon. For one, Godspeed did not love Perpetua, and this lack
of feeling was reciprocated. He was the oppressor who appeared
from nowhere, the stranger with whom she had exchanged not
one word before he won her father's consent. At eighteen she was

hungry for games of love, while he, thirty-four and employed in a stodgy profession, was an old man already. As the day of the wedding approached, Perpetua contemplated running away, embarking on hunger strike, or giving her virginity to Furo Fiberesima, her high school classmate and the youngest of her wooers, the man she would have married if she had a choice. But she pushed off a decision until the big day arrived, then walked up the aisle on the arm of a proud father. (As they approached the altar she thought she felt her courage hardening, but her father, unknowing, whispered to her with a glaze in his eyes that in her gown she looked exactly like her mother, who surely was smiling down from heaven on this happy day. Under her veil Perpetua's face settled into a mask as stiff as a corpse.) In minutes it was done, they were declared man and wife, and she held up her face for the lifting of the veil, squeezed her eyes shut for their first kiss.

The couple set off on their honeymoon straight from the venue of the wedding reception. The trip to the international airport in Lagos, and the long flight to London, was borne in silence. The fact of her new position was brought home to the bride by the surrealness of having her passport handed back to her with a "Welcome and have a nice stay, *Mrs. Anabraba,*" and this was followed by the whirl of emotions—relief, anxiety, puzzlement—as she noticed that their luggage was carried into separate hotel rooms. That night, for their first date, her husband took her to the restaurant of their hotel. Dinner was accompanied by candles and soft music, but also by the chatter of the other diners, whose frank stares at the black pair so discomfited the bride that as she bent to eat her soup a teardrop fell into it, rippling the surface.

"Don't reward these racist pigs with your tears," her husband said. His voice was calm, and his gaze, when she raised her eyes, was steady. He dabbed his lips with the edge of his napkin, took a sip of wine. "When I remember some of the things I endured when I was in university here, like the time . . ."

The drone of his conversation made her feel like a married woman. She straightened her shoulders, removed her elbows from the table, and ignoring everybody except the man who sat before her, dining like a presiding king, she enjoyed her meal.

After dinner, they retired. Her husband walked her to her room, took the key from her to unlock the door, and handed it back. With a kiss on the cheek, he bid her good night.

She was unhooking her dinner gown when she noticed the tightness in her chest, the frantic pace of her heart. "Traitor," she murmured, tracing the curve of her left breast with a forefinger. As the gown slipped from her shoulders she executed a pirouette and skipped about the room, flinging off her undergarments as she clambered over the chairs, the bed, her scattered luggage. With blood pounding in her ears, she halted before the dressing-table mirror and stared at her nude body, then raised her hands and caressed her face, her arms, her soft belly, imagining *his* eyes, *his* fingertips, *his* lips, her pores blooming with sensation. The strength of this feeling stirred the ashes of another, and she tried to remember what was tugging at her happiness like tissue paper dangling from a shoe heel. She remembered the anxious smile on Furo Fiberesima's face when he confessed his love on the night of the graduation dance.

"Traitor! Traitor! Traitor!" she hissed at her reflection, and clapping both hands to her mouth, she spun away from the mirror.

A hot shower restored her good sense. As part of preparations for bed, she dabbed perfume behind her ears, on her neck, between her breasts. She slipped on a gauzy pink nightgown that before this night she would not have had the courage to be seen admiring in a shop window. Then she jumped into bed, pulled the covers to her chin, and waited for the knock on the door. She waited for so long that her terror that it would come changed to a foreboding that it wouldn't, and when it didn't, she cried herself to sleep.

She woke up alone in bed the next morning, still the same person, joined in marriage and yet not, not yet, her whole life ahead of her, a white heatless sun shining on her face. She sang in the shower, she hummed as she pomaded and powdered and primped, and when he knocked, she danced to the door and threw it open. Her husband reacted to her gaiety with a wide smile, and offering her his arm, he led her downstairs to breakfast.

A week later the honeymoon was over, the newlyweds returned to Nigeria, but Godspeed still did not exert his conjugal rights. By this time Perpetua's gratefulness had given way to suspicion, which grew fatter every day on a terror she nursed, that instead of the Bluebeard she feared she had married, she'd fallen into the clutches of something less than a man.

In other details, Mrs. Anabraba's life was perfect. She was mistress of a five-bedroom house in one of the choicest locales of Poteko—a district formerly known as Royal Palm Hills but renamed after independence Ogbunabali Flats, where the colonial bureaucrats had clustered their mansions and recreation clubs connected by a crisscross of palm-lined boulevards. As a child of the village, a nursling of open spaces, Perpetua adored her front garden with its coffee rose and potted poinsettia and stone-lined fishpond, its allamanda hedges and bamboo garden chairs. At the back of the house more plants, a shaded grove of fruit trees; and a kitchen garden in the corner, planted and tended by her. She had a cook, a housemaid, a servants' bell in every room. Her request to redecorate the house, which was furnished in the taste of a gentleman's club, was denied, but she was granted permission to shop for as much furniture as needed to remodel her bedroom. There was no end of grumbling from the cook—a Fante man named Yaw Kakari who had worked for the Scottish bachelor who was the previous occupier of the estate—as she set about stamping her authority on the kitchen, the only part of the house where she felt she could disobey her husband's order. She took an inventory of all the tableware, kitchen utensils, and food provisions. She had the kitchen walls—which were painted colonial white, like the rest of the house—redone in pastel green. She replaced the old gas cooker with one that had an electric hot plate and inbuilt oven. To register his displeasure at the overthrow of the old order, Yaw Kakari burnt the first pot of roast pork he prepared in the new oven.

The final affront for the old cook was when Perpetua, looking into the kitchen one Sunday morning as he prepared spaghetti and meatballs for lunch, asked him to adjust his menu to allow for Kalabari food. She was still speaking when Yaw Kakari threw down his spatula and flung off his apron, then marched to the master's study to hand in his resignation. Godspeed refused to accept it, and as a compromise, he warned his wife away from the kitchen.

৪১

In the first weeks of their marriage, Godspeed came home from work every evening with a present for his wife: a string of coral beads, a length of akwete fabric, a box of American chocolates. After handing over these gifts and observing in silence her expressions of delight, he would retire to his bedroom to freshen up, and from there to his study. Except when Perpetua, feeling like an intruder, went in to interrupt his work, they would not set eyes on each other again until Yaw Kakari rang the bell for dinner. By the third week after their return from their honeymoon the presents had stopped coming, but the domestic pattern was established.

In this trying time, Perpetua discovered that the one true friend she had was the housemaid, Tenemenam. What drew them together at first was the suspicion the young bride harbored that her husband was getting his sexual needs fulfilled in Tene's bed. This specter was raised when she disclosed her troubles to her committee of friends. That day, a rainy Monday that seemed perfect for such confessions—rain lashed the windowpanes, lightning seared the cold, heavy air—a deep silence fell on the room after the words left her mouth. Then Tene walked in with a tray of refreshments balanced in her arms. When she left, Judith, one of Perpetua's oldest friends, cleared her throat and spoke.

"Your husband is fucking that girl, you fool."

The truth of these words struck Perpetua hard. It was obvious, like day after night, this solution to a conundrum that had given her sleepless nights. An answer that had been there all the while, that greeted her with bogus respectfulness every morning, and served her tea and biscuits with a mocking smile tucked behind that obsequious mask—yet she hadn't seen it. But her eyes were now opened, the truth was revealed, she could see clearly. Outside, the storm raged on.

Against the counsel of her friends, who urged her to dismiss the housemaid without delay, Perpetua decided to get closer to her rival, to know her better in order to uncover her plan. She set about this task with a resolve that surprised her—one would think she was in love with the man! Her opening move was to insinuate herself into Tene's confidence. On the Friday after her friends' visit, which was housecleaning day, she picked up a broom and mop and joined Tene in cleaning the house. The housemaid saw her madam's action as a roundabout way of expressing dissatisfaction with her work, and so Perpetua's initial attempts at establishing camaraderie—What's your favourite color? Who do you think is the better singer, Bobby Benson or Cardinal Rex? Major Nzeogwu has fine eyes, don't you agree?—were like fetching water from a stream with a raffia basket. But, with persistence, Perpetua prevailed. By the time they moved upstairs to clean the master bedroom, Tene, in fulfillment of a long-held desire to be on convivial terms with a mistress she secretly admired, had capitulated to Perpetua's overtures.

They chatted as they worked. Then Perpetua—who was carrying a stack of newspapers across the room—said in a low, confidential voice: "Do you know my friend Judith? She was here on

Monday, the one wearing those ugly camelhair shoes. Anyway, Judith is seeing a married man."

"Chei! Poor woman!"

Perpetua stopped abruptly. The newspaper pile swayed in her arms, then crashed to the ground. She turned to face Tene. "What do you mean, *poor* woman? Judith?"

"No o! The man wife."

"I see." Pe rpetua dipped her head, stared at the floor, and then knelt to gather the newspapers. By the time she rose with the load she had recovered the thread of her thoughts. "Anyway, I've warned Judith, one day this thing will blow up in her face."

"Ah auntie, to tell you truth, all this township women like that kind of thing o. E get this one woman I sabe, she dey do am with her sistah husband. Her own blood sistah!"

"Imagine."

They were making the bed when Perpetua, having laid the groundwork, began her investigation in earnest. "Tene," she said, as she stooped to take hold of one end of the sheet, "I want to tell you—take that side, oya, shake!—a secret." The bed sheet billowed between them. They spread it out and tucked in the edges. "You know I see you as a friend," Perpetua continued, "so this, what I'm about to tell you, is just between me and you. Understand?"

"Yes, auntie."

The bed was finished. Perpetua straightened up. Then leaning forward, her gaze fixed on Tene's face, she said, "My husband has *never*—" her voice caught with emotion, she cleared her throat, "—seen my nakedness."

"No!" Tene exclaimed. "Auntie!"

"Yes," Perpetua said, staring at the housemaid with an intensity that frightened the girl, "we have never shared a bed!"

Tene slapped her palms together, puckered her lips, and wondered why her mistress gazed at her with that odd expression of disappointment and relief.

Perpetua was confused. What she sought in the housemaid's face was not what she saw there. She was looking for signs of contrived emotion, but she found none; she had hoped to find glee, but she saw only pity. Still, she reasoned, her failure to find what she wanted only confirmed that her opponent was wilier than she had expected.

Over the following days, all of Perpetua's efforts to disprove the housemaid's innocence (one of which was creeping to the door of her husband's bedroom in the dead of night and crouching there until sleep forced her to stagger back to bed) worked to the opposite effect. By the time she gave up the motive for which she sought out the housemaid's company at all times of day and night, she and Tene had become friends.

It was Tenemenam who brought an end to the impasse between husband and wife. With the skill of a woman who had bred goats and chickens all her life, and armed with the knowledge that jealousy is one of the foundation stones of love, Tene took on the task of bringing the couple together. She used her intimacy with Perpetua to arouse Godspeed's curiosity; she led her into displaying signs of affection in his presence—a quick touching of hands, an exchange of smiles, a whispered conference in an open doorway, all of which Perpetua innocently partook in. Curiosity, with time, turned to suspicion, and the bridge between suspicion and jealousy, in matters of the heart, is the imagination, so Godspeed found himself in the ignominious position of jealous husband.

᪥

Godspeed got what he sought from marriage: the respectability that comes with renouncing bachelorhood; a connection with a reputable family; a wife who was as pretty as any of those pampered creatures that at the height of his poverty he had in equal measure been intimidated by and attracted to. "But something . . . something's missing." He admitted this to himself on the first night of his honeymoon, as he prepared to go in to a woman who wasn't a stranger only because she had said "I do." That "something" he refused to give the name *love*. Not love, that indefinable word, that plaything on the lips of adolescents and roués alike. Godspeed was a self-made man—he knew what was what. It was not love that had picked him from the gutter, no.

"It was hard work," he muttered, pacing back and forth before his bride's hotel room door. It was hard work that put him through school and got him his house and his position in polite society, and yes, it was hard work, not love, that would close the gulf between him and the woman who bore his name. Having struck on this resolution, he retired for the night.

&

On the day of the second coup d'état, the last Friday in July 1966, Godspeed Anabraba, like other civil servants across the country, closed early from work, and returned home to find that his wife and his housemaid had left the house without leaving word of their destination. Faced with his master's anger, Yaw Kakari forgot his grudge and tried to protect Perpetua, but the truth came out. It was not the first or second time that the two women had gone out together.

Eight minutes before the start of the curfew, Godspeed heard the clang of the gate closing, followed moments later by the excited voices of his wife and housemaid. He was sitting in his study, in his leather swivel chair, and a newspaper lay open, unread, in his lap. He stopped himself from rushing out to confront his wife. He would not give her the satisfaction of seeing how much her betrayal hurt him. He would wait for her to come and explain her guilt. The sounds that entered his study were like pricks to an open wound; his wife's voice thrummed with a vivacity he had never noticed before. As she approached the study door he raised the newspaper to his face, but the next moment he flung it away.

His wife had passed the study. Her voice, as she hummed a barracks tune under her breath, receded up the stairs.

Godspeed decided that Tenemenam must leave his house, immediately, the next morning, after the curfew; but that was the easy part. He spent hours in the unlit study—without his dinner, as he ordered away everyone who knocked on the door—pacing the floor like a caged hyena, niggled by his fear of failure. When the hallway grandfather clock struck the first chime of eleven, he rose and rushed out of the study.

The eleventh stroke rang through the sleeping house as Godspeed, panting from the dash upstairs, pushed open his wife's bedroom door. He stood in the doorway, tried to suppress the boiler room tumult of his breath, and then stepped into the darkness of that room, which he hadn't entered since his wife moved in. Apart from the swish of the ceiling fan, there was no sound. He padded toward the bed, his fury held at the ready, like a poised whip. His shin struck a chair's edge, and he halted, listening, watching for signs of life. Nothing stirred. He started forward, reached the bed, groped along the headboard, and snapped on the bedside lamp.

Perpetua was curled on her side, one arm slung across the pillow, the other tucked under her cheek, the coverlet gathered about her waist. Her chest heaved and fell with tidal rhythm; her breath warmed the air. She wore a pale yellow nightdress, and her breasts, visible through the sheer fabric, sagged with heaviness.

Godspeed gazed long at the sleeping woman, and felt his anger fade. Her beauty struck him with remorse. Yes, he had wronged her, and yes, he was sure, he was wrong about her. He switched off the light, turned to leave, and then changed his mind, dropped to his knees beside the bed and stroked her cheek, his breath mingling with hers. His hand moved to her neck, caressed her collarbone. When his fingers brushed her breast her sharp intake of breath confirmed what he knew, that she had awoken when the light came on.

"Perpetua."

"Mm?"

"I'm sorry."

"Mm." She stretched her arms wide and arched like a stroked cat.

They kissed with their eyes open. And when Godspeed, sucking her lips like a drowning man, pushed her thighs apart and entered her, Perpetua noticed, over the stab of pain, that his eyes shone in the dark with a soft luster.

ॐ

True to his pledge, Godspeed Anabraba, faced with the charge of nursing his infant daughter through her illness, did not fail. He drafted a squad of pediatricians and chose which of their recommendations to administer. He sat day and night by the child's bedside, to monitor who was winning the battle of wills. He was repaid for his alertness on the second day of his vigil, as a coughing bout that seemed harmless at first but revealed its true nature by its persistence almost choked her to death. It was late at night, he was heavy-limbed with sleep, but obeying his suspicions, he rose to turn on the light and saw his daughter's inflated face scrunched up in a grimace as she choked on a regurgitated mess of food and medicine. She was in the final throes, but fighting, the brave child. Her hands were pressed into tiny fists, which hovered over her face, a parody of rage. Godspeed let out a yell that reverberated through the night (it made Tene assume the worst and begin to howl in mourning, without rising from sleep), and then he rushed to the crib, lifted the child, flipped her upside down and slapped her back until her gasps changed to piercing wails.

After her breathing calmed, he fetched a towel, soaked it in the basin of water that stood on the redwood dresser, and cleaned her down. Her head was as tender as a blister; he discovered the meaning of gentleness as he wiped the vomit from her nostrils and mouth. He held her against his chest and swayed from side to side until she quivered with snores. He found he couldn't let go of her, this life that he had snatched from the cliff edge of oblivion. Clutching her eggshell frame to his gurgling belly, he settled into his swivel chair and fell asleep.

When he opened his eyes in the morning the first thing he noticed was that the whole world smelled of baby poop. Then he saw that his daughter's head had returned to normal size. He leaped up from the chair with a shout, which startled the child awake, and he spent the next few minutes soothing her angry wails and parrying the machine-gun questions that Tene and Yaw Kakari shot at him. In the midst of this confusion, he suddenly experienced a moment of calm, an ecstatic lightness of being. In that corner room of his consciousness he came face to face with the knowledge that sometime during the night, when he was at his most defenseless in sleep, love had crept up on him. The third thing he noticed was the leaden feeling that nestled at the bottom of his joy. For it was only now, after she had got past the worst, that Godspeed began to fear for his daughter's life.

アン

On the morning she departed the Citadel, Perpetua told herself, over and over again on the journey homeward, that her prayer had been answered. But beneath the bombast of belief she still expected the worst. God worked in mysterious ways, and even as she pleaded her case, she was ready to accept that his decision could not be overturned.

When she entered the nursery and saw the baby, cured of her misshapen head and sleeping in her father's arms, she shouted with surprise and ran to seize her. She pressed her face into the baby's hair and sniffed in the pure, cleansing smell of infant well being. But even as she cooed with joy the thought ran through her mind: who was responsible for this miracle? Who had fasted and prayed and gone without sleep for three whole days? Who had given her

life to Christ so that her child's might be saved? Perpetua turned
to her silent husband, dropped to her knees, raised the howling,
squirming baby, Daoju Anabraba, high above her head, and burst
into hosannas.

· 2 ·

Daoju was two years old when Yaw Kakari, the cook, died in
his sleep. Tenemenam found his stiffened body in the morning
when she entered his room in the boys' quarters to ask why the
master's breakfast was not ready. He lay in bed, uncovered, on his
back. He wore a green satin pajama suit that was several sizes too
large. His eyes were glazed over; his carefully manicured hands
were hooked into claws; his yellowed teeth, which had begun to
fall out when he turned seventy-four, peeped through his black,
pruned lips.

Hearing the housemaid's shouts, Godspeed came downstairs in
his housecoat to see what the matter was. Tene sobbed and snorted
phlegm as she blurted the news to him. In astonished silence he
hurried to the boys' quarters. By the time Tene arrived with his
sleepy-eyed wife he had covered the corpse with the thin gray blanket he'd found on the bed. He ordered Tene to hush up and go upstairs to keep his daughter in her room, and asked his wife—who
was kneeling beside the bed and murmuring into her hands—to
shorten her prayer so she could go and telephone the police. While
his instructions were carried out, he searched the room for docu-
ments that would reveal the addresses of Yaw Kakari's next of kin,
but found none.

Yaw Kakari was buried in College Hospital Cemetery. Wood
was in short supply because of the civil war, and his coffin was constructed from doors and broken furniture scavenged from abandoned houses. Apart from two gravediggers who, as they shoveled
clods into the hole, chattered in Ikwerre about the Biafran army

retreat, Godspeed and Perpetua were the only people who attended the funeral.

ॐ

With Yaw Kakari's death, Perpetua took over the kitchen. After she had accepted Jesus Christ as her lord and savior and began devoting two days of the week to church activities, her relationship with the old cook had gotten better. He approved of her sacrifice; he liked that though she was young and married and rich, despite the temptations of her position, she had turned her attention to the afterlife. He was Anglican, but he hadn't attended service in more than the thirty years that he'd lived in Nigeria, so he wasn't Anglican anymore, as Perpetua argued each time she asked him to accompany her to the Citadel. He demurred—he wasn't ready, he was too busy, he was too old to change his ways.

Many afternoons and evenings, while Yaw Kakari prepared lunch or dinner, and Daoju napped or played in the garden under Tene's care, and Godspeed was at the office or in his study, Perpetua hung about the kitchen, chatting with the cook. She described her church members in detail, discussed the pastor's homilies, talked about war and weather and what to wear, and yet managed always to retain an undercurrent of sermonizing. Yaw Kakari could not withstand her Bible quoting, and five weeks before he died, he was baptized at the Citadel.

It was Tene that Perpetua first tried to convert, but whenever religion found its way into their conversation, the housemaid would fall silent and hang her head. In response to Perpetua's invitations to the Citadel, Tene said, every time, "Ah, auntie!" or "I no sure o, auntie," or "You serious, auntie?" Perpetua did not give up because a Christian cannot lose hope, but after several months of receiving the same rebuffs, she lost the zeal to save Tene's soul.

Over the years their friendship cooled. Perpetua's relations with her husband settled into a pattern she could endure, and she was not as needy for an ally in her home. Also, she had a child now, who demanded her attention. Her church activities, too, kept her busy. Three years of marriage had given her the confidence to lower her regard for the housemaid. She accepted that Tene, who had two lovers in the city and a fiancé in the village, was the more experienced woman. But she, Perpetua, was educated; Tene was not. She was married; Tene was not. She had a child; Tene did not. And, most important, she was in touch with God, and Tene, because of her stubbornness, her stealing, her lies, was going to hell.

Perpetua had reason to suspect that Tene was a thief. Since Yaw Kakari's death, she had begun to notice that foodstuff went missing from the kitchen. One yam, some onions, a few cups of palm oil, a tin of curry powder, little things that added up to a truth she dreaded. Then the matchstick that she set on the rice bucket was moved. After that trap was sprung she challenged Tene in Godspeed's presence, but the housemaid broke down in tears and swore on her great-grandfather's grave that she had never stolen a pin from the Anabrabas. Godspeed believed her.

He was the problem. He was not saved, he did not attend church, he forbade Christian conversation in his presence. He refused to allow their daughter to attend the Citadel, which in a moment of anger he called a "congregation of money-grabbers" and a "temple of charlatans." Their biggest fight was sparked by these insults. Their longest-running was over his shameless hogging of their daughter's affection.

Instances. He put Daoju to bed every night, because she wouldn't sleep unless he read her a bedtime story. To break this habit Perpetua had begged her daughter, bribed her with sweets, threatened her with spankings, even put her in prayer. But until her father squeezed into her bed and clasped her to his chest as he described the antics of witches and water spirits and talking animals, the child wouldn't sleep. Ever since Daoju learned to walk, in the mornings, sometimes before dawn stained the sky, she rose from her bed and tottered across the upstairs hallway into theirs. It was disturbing behavior for a girl, this attachment to her father's bed, Perpetua thought every time it happened. Whenever she heard the door creak open and felt the mattress sag under her daughter's weight, she lost her sleep. When she complained that these morning visits ruined her day, her husband told her to move back to her old bedroom, if she preferred. She did not.

It was the same with food: Godspeed had to be there. When he was, the child followed him to the table and fed herself, imitating his actions, hungry for his approval. When he wasn't, feeding her was an ordeal, a mud fight of tears and spilled food and clashing wills. Weekday lunch was the hardest: the struggle to make her eat always ended in defeat or hard-fought victory, which felt the same.

"Time to eat, Daoju."

"Where's daddy?"

"He's at the office. Come here."

"No."

"Come, *please*."

"No-no-no-no-NO!"

"Come, *now*, before I smack your bottom!" Tears, grudging approach, and then trouble. She wanted everything except what she was given. If boiled yam was placed before her, she wanted onunu, the mash of yam, ripe plantain, and palm oil. If her plate held onunu, she wanted dodo. If fried plantain was what she met at the table, she wanted jollof rice. If leftovers were in the fridge and Perpetua asked Tene to warm some up, then her tactics changed, and the food became too hot or too much or too ugly or too full of dead ants. At that point, depending on her mood or her plans for the day, Perpetua handed the problem over to Tene.

Sometimes, when she saw how the child's eyes lit up whenever her father entered the room, when she sat with her family and felt as if her face was pressed against the glass, stuck on the outside while their love blazed on the other side, Perpetua admitted to herself that she had lost her daughter. She knew when it happened, and she knew why. It was her husband's fault, he had stolen their daughter's love; he wanted to punish her because she had found God, who saved her child. But the knowledge brought no comfort.

Like Job, her faith was being tested. Why else—despite all her efforts, which would continue for fifteen years; despite her prayers, her night vigils, her holy water douches, the careful observance of her ovulation periods, when, even if he was tired, she stroked and crooned and kissed her husband into submission, and then, after he collapsed on her, she remained with her legs raised, wrapped around his back, just so nothing would be wasted, every single drop would have a fighting chance of breaking her womb's defense—could she not get pregnant? A fresh start, another child, would help her endure her husband and daughter's fondness for each other. Otherwise, she foresaw a future where she would forever be the minority in a vote of three, always the odd one out.

ᛒᛣ

The big fight happened on a Friday in May 1970, four months after the civil war ended. That night, in the dining room, husband and wife traded insults in front of their daughter, in front of their housemaid, and in front of his friends, colleagues from the office who had come to dinner. Above the cries of Daoju and the pleas of their guests, the couple shouted at each other, shot out of their chairs and pointed fingers, then advanced, flinging words like daggers. Then Perpetua grabbed her husband by the shirtfront and screeched in his face, "Kill me now, you demon!" and Godspeed, for the first and last time in their eighteen years together, raised his hand against his wife. He struck her, once, across the mouth.

The day had started well. Perpetua, as usual, rose early to fix breakfast while her husband and daughter prepared for work and school, and then she joined them at the table, which was not her usual practice. Every Friday for the past two months she had played host to Mr. Farasin, a church member who Bible studied with her and exorcised the house; so, on that day, she was in an expectant mood. She snapped at Daoju to stop playing with her fried egg yolk and to drink up her Horlicks or her father would leave her behind, yet when her daughter rose from the table, despite leaving the egg half-eaten and the drink untouched, she smiled at her, happy to see her go. As Daoju tripped to the sitting room to collect her school backpack and lunch box, Godspeed, dangling his car keys in one hand, his Samsonite brown leather briefcase clutched in the other, walked to the front door, followed by his wife. They stopped in the open doorway, stood side by side, their arms touching, both of them silent, lost in thought. Then they drew apart so Daoju could pass between them. Godspeed bent forward to kiss his wife's cheek, and he told her, "I forgot to mention—I invited four colleagues over for dinner tonight. Three you haven't met and Goodnews Abrakasa, who might bring along one of his wives. We'll arrive together, seven-ish."

Perpetua nodded, her forehead drawn in a frown of concentration, and kept on nodding, her vacant eyes staring at the receding shapes of her husband and daughter. When the car engine vroomed she started awake, and then pulled the front door closed and hurried up the stairs.

Mr. Farasin arrived promptly at ten. Tene let him in, and after she called her mistress, she headed to the boys' quarters to hide in her room. Perpetua entered the sitting room to find him slouched in an armchair, his long thin thighs splayed, thumbing through her wedding photo album. He swung his legs closed and stood up to greet her. Then he raised the photo album and faced it to her, his fingers gripping the top. With the other hand he pointed out her husband's photo and said, "This is your husband."

"Yes," Perpetua said.

"The Lord Jehofah has planned big things for him. Don't worry, we will get him."

"Amen," said Perpetua.

Tall and skinny, with a shaved head, a skull-like face, roaming yellow eyes, and a feeble mustache, Mr. Farasin only wore dull-colored polyester safari suits. His color today was bottle-green. His feet were tucked in black, cracked leather shoes as long as scuba flippers. His vinyl attaché case, stamped on the flap with the Citadel's emblem, a cathedral ringed by fire and crowned with a halo, was always by his side, in his hand, on his lap, where it served as a lectern for his bulging, finger-stained Bible. His voice was a vibrant bass. He spoke English with a thick Oyo accent, which meant his *vex* was pronounced *fex,* his *charm* became a *sham,* and on a sunny day, the "shun sown."

Perpetua asked him to sit. She walked to the drinks cabinet to fetch a bottle of Lucozade and two glasses. She poured a glass for him and the other for herself, then picked up her Bible from the center table and settled into the armchair beside him. After the usual chitchat, which lasted as long as the energy drink in their glasses, they got down to business.

"Let us pray," Mr. Farasin said. Perpetua bowed her head, and he began, slowly at first, then faster, angrier. Perpetua's responses grew louder, matching his rising intensity. His face, which shone with sweat, took on the character of his words—when he slew enemies and collapsed obstacles and taunted the devil, his face grimaced; and when he said, "Our lives are in your hands, O Lord, do with us as you wiss," his shoulders sagged, his features slackened, became submissive. The prayer ended with the request that God grant his two servants the wisdom to understand the Bible passages that he had chosen for them today. Then Mr. Farasin opened his eyes, Perpetua opened her eyes; Mr. Farasin opened his Bible, Perpetua opened her Bible; Mr. Farasin selected a passage, read, and explained, Perpetua listened.

After Bible study, it was time to rid the house of demons. Perpetua rose from her seat and went into the visitors' toilet to collect the bucket of tap water she had asked Tene to stand there. She placed the bucket in front of Mr. Farasin, and then picked a bottle of anointed oil from the center table. She had a cache of extra virgin olive oil in the wardrobe of the smaller, unused guest room, whose furniture was from the time of Mr. McGee, the colonial administrator who had lived in the house before them. Every Sunday Perpetua took a new bottle to church for the pastor to consecrate. Once the bottle was opened for her Friday prayer sessions, the leftover content was sent to the kitchen for use as cooking oil.

She approached Mr. Farasin. He stood up, accepted the bottle from her, broke the seal, and uncapped it, and then poured a dollop of oil into the water. Stirring the water, he said in a ringing voice: "By the power of God Jehofah, king of kings and lord of lords, protector of the innocent and destroyer of enemies, I sanctify this water in Jesus' name!"

"Amen!" Perpetua shrieked, waving her Bible over her head.

Mr. Farasin scooped a handful of water. "Out, out, out—blood of Jesus!" he yelled, as he flung out his arm. Water flew across the room and spattered the wall, the ceiling, the glass door of the drinks cabinet. "In the name of Jesus, get out!" he shouted, and threw water again.

"O yes Jesus, yes Lord!" Perpetua cried.

She trailed Mr. Farasin as he walked through the house. He knew the house well; he had gone over it several times. He threw open the bedroom doors as if he didn't expect to find anyone there. He burst into the bathrooms and splashed water on the folded towels and drying underwear. He leaned into kitchen cupboards and sprinkled the grain sacks, the empty pots, the drowsing geckos. Five bedrooms, four bathrooms, two sitting rooms, one dining room, one study, one kitchen, one pantry, three balconies, and one verandah—they went everywhere.

They returned to the downstairs sitting room a half hour later, both of them dappled with sweat and holy water. "Thank you,

Jesus," Perpetua said, wiping her brow with her hand. "Thank you, Lord," Mr. Farasin said. Perpetua's voice was hoarse; Mr. Farasin's was unaffected. With a sigh of exhaustion Perpetua dropped into a chair, and Mr. Farasin said, "We hafen't finished, madam. The Lord has refealed to me that there is a place in this house where the agents of Satan are still hiding."

Perpetua sat up. "Where?"

"Where does your house girl sleep?"

"Ah, that's true!" Perpetua exclaimed, and leaped to her feet. "Come, come with me!"

A cobbled path led from the kitchen door to the boys' quarters. Perpetua walked in front; Mr. Farasin followed at a pace that made her turn her head and throw him impatient looks. It was his first time in this part of the compound. He gazed at the trees, the pawpaw, the mango, the guava, the dwarf coconut, the clump of banana. The largest tree in the yard, a false almond tree, grew in front of the boys' quarters—its massive branches formed a green canopy over the roof, casting the red brick structure in shadow. The ground under the tree, around the boys' quarters' verandah was pebbled with rotting fruit, which scented the air.

Perpetua climbed the verandah and waited for Mr. Farasin. In her haste she had left behind her Bible. Mr. Farasin clutched his in one hand. The bucket, with water sloshing inside, was held in the other.

The boys' quarters had four doors. The bathroom door had rotted off its hinges; it leaned against the wall. The kitchen door hung open to reveal a soot-blackened ceiling, a coal brazier, a large enamel basin of fermenting tapioca. The third door, which bore a Citadel sticker, was padlocked. The last door was closed. When Mr. Farasin stepped onto the verandah, Perpetua walked to the last door and pushed it open.

The room, though sparsely furnished, was cluttered. A metal bed faced the door, and a row of cartons lay in the thick dust collected under it. Beside the bed stood the old cooker that Perpetua had replaced nearly three years ago; its closed lid was covered with cosmetic bottles and tubes, skeins of glass bead jewelry, combs, hairpins, hairbrushes. In front of the cooker was a straight-backed chair, which was draped with clothes. A raffia bag stood against one wall of the room, and clothes spilled from its mouth. The floor was scattered with high-heel shoes, leather sandals, cloth slippers, candy-colored pom-poms. Perpetua stood in the doorway and stared at the disorder. She recognized many of the clothes and footwear, the heart-shaped jar of face lotion that she had thrown away because it lightened her skin, a chipped crock water jug that was a wedding present from someone she couldn't remember, the wooden hairbrush that broke in half when she flung it at a cockroach. Tene's room, to Perpetua's astonished gaze, was a house of mirrors constructed out of her memories.

Tene lay on her back on the bed, her knees raised and her skirt gathered around her waist. A transistor radio, playing highlife music, sat on her belly. At Perpetua's entry she turned a surprised face toward the door, and when Mr. Farasin appeared she sat up and arranged her skirt, then swung her legs off the bed. The radio crashed to the floor and fell silent.

"Auntie?" Tene said in an anxious voice. Her eyes watched Mr. Farasin.

"We have come to cleanse your room," Perpetua said.

"Ehn?"

"You heard her," Mr. Farasin said. "Your room has evil spirits."

Gloom settled over Tene's face. She sighed deeply, then rose from the bed and took a step toward the door, but Mr. Farasin turned and pulled it shut.

"You stay," he said.

Tene glanced at Perpetua, who dropped her eyes; then she returned her gaze to Mr. Farasin, glared at him. "I be Roman Catholic."

"God is God anywhere," Mr. Farasin said.

He held her gaze. She remained silent. Then he stuck his Bible under his arm, raised the bucket, asked the women to kneel and close their eyes. Tene refused with a shake of her head, and sat at the bed's edge to watch him. He nodded at Perpetua. After Perpetua knelt and bent her head, he began to pray and spray water. His voice rose; it beat the air. He placed his wet hand on Perpetua's forehead, and she swayed, gasped for breath. He released her and strode toward Tene with his hand outstretched, but she moved her head away from his grasp. He bent down, set the bucket on the floor, then grabbed Tene's shoulder with his left hand to restrain her, and when she raised her face in protest, he gripped her temples with his right. She struggled, and he held on, chanting prayers. His fingers squeezed until she groaned and beat his arm with her fists. He released her, and she sank to the floor, her legs kicking. Her foot caught the transistor radio. It slid across the floor, struck the wall, and burst into music.

"Amen!" Mr. Farasin shouted.

"Amen!" Perpetua cried, and opened her eyes.

Mr. Farasin removed the Bible from under his arm, touched it to his forehead, left shoulder, then right. He said, "You can get up now, madam. Your house is clean."

As Tene struggled onto her knees, Perpetua rose to her feet. Mr. Farasin put his arm round her shoulder and led her toward the door. In the doorway, he turned around.

"You," he said in a stern, booming voice, pointing his Bible at Tene, "if you want to remain in this house, you must change your church."

Tene's breath rasped in her throat. "Who you be to tell me—"

"Shut up, thief," Perpetua said.

෨

With a gift of eighty shillings, Mr. Farasin left. When the gate clanged shut behind him, Perpetua rang the bell for Tene. They had not begun cooking when the school bus honked at the gate. Tene led Daoju upstairs, changed her clothes, then piggybacked her to the dining table and sat with her as Daoju struggled through lunch. The meal finished, she took her to the garden to play for half an hour, and then carried her kicking and screaming to her bedroom for siesta. By the time Tene returned to the kitchen, pots were bubbling on the cooker, the air was thick with the aroma of roasted chicken and groundnut stew and coconut rice, and Perpetua was standing at the sink, skinning a pineapple.

Daoju rose from sleep at twenty-one minutes past three. At two minutes to four, Perpetua sent Tene to Aunty Deborah Store, which was just round the corner, to buy a crate of beer. While Tene discharged the errand, Perpetua set Daoju on her knee and read to her from the Bible, from chapter thirty of Exodus, which was as far as they had gone in two months of daily reading. The plan, undertaken on the advice of Mr. Farasin, was to read the entire Bible to her daughter before her third birthday. It was slow going; Daoju found the stories bewildering, dreary. Before long—as happened whenever her mother insisted on this ritual—she began to scratch her elbows, and pull her Calabar plaits, and swing her legs with impatience. When she interrupted to ask if she could go outside to play, Perpetua lost her temper.

"You've started again, you stubborn child! You're lucky I don't have time for you today! No more play—go into your room and stay there!"

Daoju climbed the stairs, sobbing.

At seventeen minutes past four, Tene returned. After stacking beer in the refrigerator, she asked Perpetua where Daoju was. A cluck of annoyance was the reply she got. She mumbled an excuse and slipped from the kitchen, but halted on the staircase when Perpetua called out, "Leave her alone. Go and bathe and change into something nice. Our visitors will be here by seven."

When the grandfather clock struck five, Perpetua went upstairs to prepare herself. At ten minutes to six, she emerged from the bedroom. She wore a cream muslin gown, a string of pearls, and silver sandals. She walked past her daughter's bedroom, down the stairs, and into the kitchen. She smiled when Tene, who was dozing on a stool, started awake and said, "Ah auntie, your cloth fine o!"

Under Perpetua's direction, Tene set the table. The tablecloth was changed. Napkins were arranged. The silverware, porcelain plates, and crystal wineglasses were unboxed, cleaned, and laid out. The food, served into lidded dishes, was moved from the kitchen to the dining room sideboard. At fifteen minutes to seven, Perpetua gave Tene last instructions. She reminded her about the refrigerated jugs of drinking water and when to serve dessert, and showed her again how to remove the plates, how to refill the wineglasses, how to walk, to bend forward, to smile.

At two minutes past seven, Godspeed arrived with the guests.

ℬↃ

Sam Briggs was a big-voiced, big-bellied man. His round cheeks oozed health and Old Spice aftershave, and he cultivated a regal air, with his arms held away from his body and his neck as stiff as a cockerel's. He wore a white voile etibo over black gabardine trousers, his dove-gray bowler hat sat at an angle over one eye, and his pointed black leather shoes were polished to a dazzle. He wore gold around his neck and left ring finger, and silver signet rings on the four fingers of his right hand, which clutched the silver knob of his ebony walking stick. Sam Briggs led the group into the house. Perpetua was waiting in the foyer. On sighting her he threw his arms wide as if for an embrace, but when he drew near he brought his hands together with a soft clap. She curtsied and held out her hand.

"Chief Samson Briggs. Enchanted to make your acquaintance, Mrs. Anabraba," he said, clasping her hand. His thumb stroked the back of her fingers. "Your husband boasts of your beauty, but his words have done you no justice. You are spectacular!"

A giggle rose to Perpetua's throat, but she fought it back, forced it into a smile. "I'm happy to meet you too, Chief Briggs," she said.

"Please call me Sam." He raised his head, sniffed the air, and grinned at Perpetua. "Your cooking skills are also not overstated, I see."

"Of course not," said Godspeed, pushing forward to stand beside Perpetua. "Now, *Your Highness,* may I introduce *my* wife to the others?"

Sam Briggs laughed, his head thrown back, his shoulders shaking, his walking stick jabbing the floor.

The woman in the group walked forward. She looked older than her male companions. She wore a lion-head-patterned velvet wrapper, a puff-sleeved lilac blouse, and no jewelry. The skin of her face was clean, devoid of makeup, and her thin, brown hair was pulled into a bun. Godspeed said, "This is Mrs. Kenule," and she reached forward to shake Perpetua's hand.

"It's a pleasure to meet you, Mrs. Kenule. I am Perpetua."

"Likewise, my dear," Mrs. Kenule said. "Your husband has been singing your praises."

"Stop giving my wife the impression that I speak only of her." Godspeed smiled down at Perpetua, then draped his right arm around her waist and raised the left in a beckoning gesture. "Boma, my wife. Perpetua, Boma Peterside."

With a swift sidelong glance at her husband, Perpetua turned to Boma Peterside. "Pleased to meet you," she said, and smiled at the ginger-haired, sea-eyed albino who came forward, nodding shyly. His handshake left a dab of sweat in her palm.

"And you've met my almost namesake," said Godspeed, inclining his head at Goodnews Abrakasa, who strode up, grasped Perpetua's shoulders, and bussed her on both cheeks.

"Welcome, Goodnews," Perpetua said, her eyes twinkling. "How come you're alone today?"

"Ah," Goodnews Abrakasa said, throwing up his hands, "it happened like this. I planned to come with Number Two wife, as Number One has been here before, but one of her children, the one who's a sickler, got malaria this morning, so she couldn't make it. Number One wife wanted to follow me, but to avoid future wahala, I refused o."

Goodnews Abrakasa was a wiry man with caterpillar eyebrows, a pimpled nose, and strong, white teeth. His face shone with good humor. He favored wide collar shirts, unbuttoned to his hairy belly; bell-bottom trousers that were tight in the crotch; and high-heeled boots. Close friends, in private conversation, called him "Big Snake."

Godspeed made a rude noise in his throat and jerked his head at Goodnews Abrakasa. "But you claim you can control your wives, don't you, Mr. Polygamist? How come then you're afraid of them?"

"Who's afraid?" Goodnews Abrakasa shot back. "When a man sees boiling water and doesn't stick in his hand, do you call that fear?"

"You two, not now," Sam Briggs said, brandishing his walking stick as he stepped forward. "Dinner is waiting." Perpetua took his offered arm. They walked toward the dining room, the others following.

॰

Godspeed sat at one end of the table, Perpetua at the other. Sam Briggs took the seat on Perpetua's right and Goodnews Abrakasa sat on her left. Tene was passing round the serving dishes when Godspeed sat bolt upright in his chair and glanced around, then raised his hand, beckoning to her. She approached his chair. "Where's my daughter?" he asked.

"She dey her room."

"Why?"

Tene looked at Perpetua, and Godspeed followed her gaze.

Perpetua, deep in conversation with Sam Briggs, was unaware of the attention.

Godspeed's eyes flared. "Drop everything you're doing and go and bring my daughter, now!" he said in a furious voice. The table fell silent.

"Yes, oga," Tene said, and left the room.

In a coaxing tone, Mrs. Kenule said to Godspeed: "I was going to ask about your daughter, but I thought she had gone to bed."

"My daughter doesn't go to sleep without first seeing me," Godspeed said. "Besides, she hasn't had her supper." He looked at Perpetua. "Is that correct?"

Perpetua nodded. Sam Briggs turned to speak to her, saw the expression on her face, and coughed into his hand.

Tene entered with Daoju in her arms. The child's eyes were tear-swollen and her face was drawn into unhappy lines. When she saw the strange faces, she clung tighter to Tene's neck. Then she caught sight of her father.

"Daddy!"

"Baby!"

Godspeed pushed back his chair and rose with opened arms. Tene handed the child to him and shuffled backward. Daoju wriggled in her father's arms, her features fluid, riven by excitement. She spoke in a rush, her voice a brook after rain, babbling.

"Daddy, Daddy . . . crying long . . . dark room . . . Bible story—"

"Sh, baby, sh, my dear, my love, sh."

Godspeed asked Boma Peterside to move seats. He set his daughter in the vacated chair, spread a napkin over her lap, then sat down and said, "Everybody, this is Daoju, my princess."

She beamed and nodded round the table, her body swaying from the force of her swinging legs. Sam Briggs called her beautiful, a budding rose, a chip off her mother's block. Boma Peterside reached his hand forward and brushed her cheek, as if to check that she was real. Mrs. Kenule asked her about her age, and when she replied, "Two years and three-quarters, thank you," the whole table except Perpetua burst into laughter.

"My dear Perpetua," Goodnews Abrakasa said loudly, "I've told your husband before and I'm telling you now, your daughter must marry one of my sons. Yes o, Godspeed, I'm staking my claim early. This girl will marry an Abrakasa."

"As long as it's your son and not you, we might consider," Perpetua said, to the amusement of everyone but her husband, who did not join in the laughter. He waited to the end of the others' raillery of Goodnews Abrakasa, and then he said: "When the time comes my daughter will marry who she pleases." He turned to Perpetua, who was staring at him with a wide, bitter gaze. "And please, my dear, don't joke about such matters in front of our daughter." He looked sideways at Daoju, smiled, pulled a funny face, and patted her head. "One more thing." He glanced across at his wife, and his jaw muscles bunched. "Daoju just told me, 'Bible story took my play.' What does that mean?"

∽

Godspeed and Perpetua, one week after their fight, were still not speaking, not sleeping in the same room or sharing mealtimes together. Daoju had become a sore in their relationship. Since her mother moved out of her father's bedroom, Daoju had taken over her mother's side of the bed. When her father returned from work in the evenings, she stuck to him; she played at his feet until her bedtime. But daytime was her mother's—the mornings when Perpetua, hot-eyed and sharp-fingered with resentment, prepared her for school, and the afternoons when she returned home to meet the cold, haggard look of maternal enmity.

∽

The following Friday, Mr. Farasin returned for the usual. Perpetua welcomed him warmly. She was lonely, unhappy, everyone was against her: her husband, her daughter, even the housemaid.

"The devil's attacks are getting stronger," she said to Mr. Farasin as he measured oil into the bucket of water. "Pour in the whole bottle, please, I'm losing my family."

"God forbid!" Mr. Farasin directed a reassuring look at her. "As long as this matter is in my hands, you will never taste defeat, don't worry."

They spent more time on the exorcism than ever before. (It will get worse before it gets better, Mr. Farasin told her, and then reassured her that in his visions she was always beside her husband, in this life and the other, so no fear of *that*.) Mr. Farasin sprinkled holy water in every corner of the house and boys' quarters, even the late cook's room, then went into the garden and sprayed the grass, the trees, the algae-covered fishpond. By the time he emptied the bucket Perpetua was tight-lipped, her eyes darting at every sound, and it was close to the hour Daoju came back home. Perpetua didn't hurry him, but she was anxious that he depart before her daughter returned. The fight with her husband was still fresh in her mind.

While Mr. Farasin stood in the sitting room, wiping his hands on his trousers, Perpetua ran up the stairs, burst into her room and grabbed some money, then dashed downstairs. Mr. Farasin was no longer where she left him. She was about to call his name when she noticed that his bag, too, was gone. That's odd, she thought, as she stared at the closed front door. Then she strode forward, picked up the glasses they had drunk from, and headed to the kitchen.

As she entered the kitchen doorway, Perpetua caught a movement, turned her head to look, and froze. Huddled in the far corner, his open attaché case clutched in one hand and in the other two sweet potatoes, was Mr. Farasin. At her gasp, he whipped his head around, and a spasm tightened his face, he seemed about to rush forward, as if to escape or to attack her. Perpetua dropped the glasses with a crash to the floor, and staggered backward.

"Mr. Farasin! What is this, what are you doing?"

He stared down at the sweet potatoes in his hand. "I'm . . . ehm . . . I was . . . ah . . ." His voice trailed off.

The truth was revealed. All this time, it had been him. "So it was you!" Perpetua shouted, stabbing her finger at him. "It was you stealing my food! But how could you, Mr. Farasin?"

Mr. Farasin dropped to his knees, his lower lip trembling. The sweet potatoes fell from his hand and bounced across the floor. His bag toppled on its side and from its open mouth rolled out onions, tomatoes, two eggs, a scattering of Maggi cubes.

"I'm sorry, ma," he begged, wringing his hands and then wiping his face with them. "Please forgive me, I didn't know what I was doing, it is the devil's work."

Perpetua's face crumpled. All lies, lies, nothing but lies! She had been deceived. She had opened her house to a snake, a thief, exposed her family. Her husband was right again: she knew what he would say when he heard of this. *Money-grabbers and charlatans,* the words that had started their fight a week ago, were nothing compared to the ones he would use. Thieves. Home breakers. The people *you* thought would save my daughter's life when *you* ran away and left her dying in my arms.

"Mr. Farasin, you have killed me," Perpetua said, her voice breathless with pain. Mr. Farasin—who was begging forgiveness with quoted Bible verses—looked up at her tone, and then crept forward on his knees. His voice rose, desperate, edged with hope. Perpetua shook her head from side to side and clamped her hands over her ears. Then she strode forward, her house slippers crunching on broken glass, and screamed at Mr. Farasin: "Get out, just get out—" and as he scrambled to his feet, grabbed up his bag and made to empty the stolen items, she flailed her arms at him, "—no, take it, take everything, just get out of my house before my daughter sees you!"

⨝

Perpetua sat in the sitting room, feet drawn together and knees apart, her hands lying on her Bible in her lap, and cried with heaving sobs. Tene bustled about her and pled for an answer. In response to her questions, Perpetua cried harder.

When Daoju returned from school to find her mother weeping, she pushed the Bible aside and climbed into her lap. She wrapped her arms around her mother's neck and pressed her lips to her wet cheek. Her daughter's clean, untainted smell, her cuddliness, made Perpetua shudder. Hugging each other tightly, they cried together. Tene stood behind them, beaming through her tears.

Godspeed arrived at evening to find the house as quiet as an empty cathedral. He asked Tene for his daughter's whereabouts, but the housemaid shrugged her shoulders and averted her eyes. In response to his next question, she said, "In your bedroom," then flashed him a look so charged with meaning that he turned away, confused.

He mounted the stairs slowly, crossed the upstairs hallway with a careful tread, and nudged open his bedroom door. The room was in darkness. As he pressed the door closed he heard the bed sheets rustle. "Don't put on the light, please," Perpetua whispered.

He could feel her stare as he walked toward the bed. "Are you ill?"

"No," she replied. "Won't you lie down?"

"But I'm a demon, isn't that what you—"

"Please, Godspeed, don't."

With a shock, Godspeed realized she was crying. He bent down quickly to set his briefcase by the armoire, and then sat on the bed and removed his shoes, his socks, his tie, his shirt and trousers. He lifted the covers and slipped in beside her in his vest and briefs. As he turned to face her she wrapped her arms and legs around him. She was naked, her skin burned. He could feel himself melting, sinking under the spell. She was different, something had changed.

"I have something to tell you," she said.

He waited, afraid to ask, to move, to spoil the moment.

"I love you," she said.

Except for the grandfather clock, which ticked in the hallway, the house was silent.

இ

The next day, the second-to-last Saturday in May 1970, the Anabrabas, father, mother, and child, dressed up and paid a visit to Banigo Bright Studios, where their happiness was caught, forever, on photographic film.

Perpetua got a phone call later that day. Judith, her best friend with whom she had lost touch at the start of the civil war, was dead. She was shot by the wife of her navy captain lover, after the woman caught them in her home. The bullet entered the back of her head and took her face along when it exited.

Perpetua flung away the receiver with a shrill scream. Tene came running, and Godspeed stood on the staircase landing and listened. Then he approached his weeping, shivering wife, put his arms around her, and said, "At least it was quick. No pain, no suffering. That's the way to go."

இ

Daoju was five years old when Tenemenam married. Her fiancé was moving to Port Harcourt to seek his fortune and Tene was sure that if she let him go alone she would never see him again. The wedding reception, planned by Perpetua and paid for by Godspeed, was held on the grounds of the Anabraba house, their parting gift and wedding present. After the good-byes, the hugs, and the promises to stay in touch, Tene climbed into the van that waited to bear her and her hoard of scavenged possessions away, and as the engine revved, as she thrust both hands out of the window and waved, Godspeed stepped forward and dropped a manila envelope thick with money into her lap. The car shot forward, trailing Tene's squeal.

That was the last they heard of her.

· 3 ·

New Year's Eve 1983, the military struck again. It was the fifth putsch the country had seen in twenty-three years of independence, and the third successful one. But this regime, it soon turned out, was unlike anything that had come before. Its leaders, like all soldiers, believed in the right of might. They had a deep aversion for corruption, for indiscipline, for all forms of opposition. They held civilians in low regard. They had a fondness for Herculean tasks and idiom, such as "cleaning out the Augean stables of our great nation" and "destroying the hydra-headed monster of corruption." They had messianic ambitions.

It was a new year, a new era, people believed, and so they gave their support to the regime. They cheered when politicians were convicted for corruption by military tribunals, when suspected criminals were executed without trial, when the civil service was purged. Given the harshness of the medicine, it was easy to believe the country would change for the better. Signs of the new season were already there: for the first time in the nation's history, her people, threatened by the whips of soldiers who enforced the regime's War against Indiscipline campaign, formed queues at bus stops.

Euphoria passed. Decrees began to rankle. Journalists, artists, and men of conscience who dared speak out were stalked and bundled into detention by secret police. The economy, burdened by debt, nosedived. In a flamboyant effort to counter currency traffickers, the color of the naira was changed, but the success of this policy was thrown in the shade by the wage cuts and lost savings and broken businesses that resulted. The constitution was suspended; labor unions were dissolved; austerity measures were adopted; the borders were closed. Apart from bus stops, long queues formed in front of banks, embassies, and supermarkets, whose shelves the importation bans had denuded. Unemployment rose, and so did crime, despite the ease with which the death penalty was applied.

University students stripped of their subsidies, public servants faced with mass retrenchment, unpaid pensioners, all took to the streets in protest. Wherever unrest appeared, it was crushed.

⟐

On the day in February 1984 that Brunei celebrated independence from Great Britain with a banquet that had 4,237 guests in attendance, fifty-one-year-old Godspeed Anabraba was compulsorily retired from the civil service. He was a permanent secretary, and he had worked for government since the early, heady days of independence, so the military authorities could not believe he wasn't corrupt. They planned to dismiss then detain him, but despite their investigations, despite the two times they raided his house—which he showed evidence of having bought from the government in 1976—and despite how far back they dug into his employment records, they could not uncover any proof of impropriety. After months of petitions, of backdoor interventions from the influential friends he had gathered in his long career, the authorities allowed him to keep a fraction of his financial assets as well as the house he lived in, but they canceled his pension and confiscated the country home he had built in his mother's honor, his bungalow in Lagos, his three cars, his scattered parcels of land, and his wife's upmarket restaurant, then sold everything off in a private auction. His offence, he was informed in a letter rife with bad spelling, was "plain for all to sea."

⟐

At sixteen, Daoju was a queen. She had the beauty, the carriage—and, in her father, the king. It was not disputed, in public or at home, that she, the child, was the love of his life. She had her father's ear, his heart, his complete trust. On days that he brought home large amounts of cash, it was into Daoju's care he placed the money. Between April 1975 and September 1983 he traveled to conferences in five European countries, one Asian, one African, and two US cities, and Daoju had accompanied him three times, Perpetua once. When relatives visited, seeking favors from the big man, it was to Daoju they directed their entreaties, it was her attention they courted. Perpetua had long since given up efforts to usurp her daughter: between mother and child there existed a fragile, unspoken truce.

Daoju adored her father. She loved him with a fierce, electric passion. He was a man; he was her model for a man. He told her everything, gave her everything. She, in turn, opened her life to him. The few secrets she kept were those she knew would embarrass him. Like the real reason she did not like red wine, because it affected her monthlies and infected her moods. Or, again, that she had never been kissed, not for lack of wooing, but because none of the men, measured against her father, was man enough.

$\gimel$

After retirement, Godspeed changed. His promise to himself had been broken. At the height of success, he had failed. His reputation had been assailed and his property stolen, and there was nothing, absolutely nothing he could do. Day after day, he sat at home, gorging himself to plumpness, watching re-reruns of British sitcoms in bed, reading the dailies in his dust-covered study, sleeping sprawled in his favorite chair with his mouth gaped open, purposeless.

Perpetua, too, after the loss of her business, her seven-year-old restaurant, remained at home. She cooked; she cleaned the house; she cried at night in her bedroom. She had good reason to grieve: her husband was a shell of himself. He had lost his spirit, his confidence; and, also, he was bleeding money. Two companies in which he held major shares had crashed. The regime's currency change had halved the value of the savings left him. When money began to run low, when the quality of life she was accustomed to could not be afforded, Perpetua, out of fear, quarreled with her husband, her daughter, her neighbors, anyone who was near. The Anabraba house became a desolate place. Favor seekers donned masks of sympathizers and trooped in like vultures, in search of pickings. Visitors dwindled, and then stopped. The large, colonial house, which once echoed with prosperity, was now as hushed as a mausoleum.

಄

Three days, one hour, and fourteen minutes before she turned seventeen, Daoju challenged her father for the first time. At 10:46 p.m. on September 8, 1984, she told him, "You're not man enough to stop me from leaving this house." Later, for the rest of her life, she realized that was the moment she killed the man who loved her most.

The day had started badly. Daoju woke up that morning to the sound of her mother hurling abuse at her father. This one-way stream of invective was a routine of late, but she usually left for school before it began. It was a Saturday; there was no excuse to leave the house early. So she lay in bed and shared her father's shame, heard his little secrets, his psychological farts. She felt trapped in a hell that was all her own. She squeezed her eyes shut, curled up under the bedcovers, and tried not to listen as her mother, spluttering with rage and tears, called her father:

a waste of time

a sad excuse for a man

a spineless failure

a stone round her neck.

He remained silent, her voice grew shriller, and she said he was:

a baboon wey dey chop when monkey dey work

a chicken

a pig

a big fat pig.

The insults seemed only to add to her mother's anguish, as her father did not reply, did not defend himself, did not rise and slap her shut. Daoju wept into her pillow.

Perpetua left the house at midday to visit her ailing father—eighty-one years old and nursing a cancerous prostate gland—whom she meant to ask for money to buy food for the house. Alone with her father, Daoju gave in to an impulse she had fought for weeks. She rolled off the bed, removed her nightgown, and rummaged in the middle drawer of the redwood dresser for what to wear, thinking of what to say to her father, all the words she would tell him to make things right again.

She entered his study to find him asleep. He was aging fast. His thick, uncombed hair and chin stubble were dusty with gray, and the wrinkles in his forehead were as deep as knife cuts. In seven months he had grown a double chin, sagging breasts, and an overhanging paunch. His breath wheezed through his wet, drooping lips.

"Daddy," she said quietly; and then bent forward to slap his knee. "Daddy!"

He twitched awake and blinked at her. He cleared his throat and swallowed, then stuck his little finger in his right ear and shook his head, his cheeks slapping. He wiped his finger on his shirtfront.

"What is it, baby?"

"Daddy, Daddy . . . Mummy . . ." Daoju said, but the look in her father's eyes, that placid stare of the broken beast, corkscrewed through her gut. She doubled over with a moan and slumped to the floor, and then began to cry, her misery a steady drizzle.

ᢒ

The day dragged for Daoju after she returned to her room. The change in her father, which she had hoped was transitory, was clearly deep-rooted. He would never again in her mind be the man he once was. To her, who had loved with all her heart what he represented—the solid, unchanging image that bore the name Daddy—this poor replica, this weakling, was an enemy, and she hated him as much as she had loved her father.

That night, in the sitting room, her mother resumed the insults. After several minutes of silent suffering, Daoju, her lips puckered into an O, rose from her seat in front of the TV and marched toward the barred front door.

"Where are you going?" Perpetua demanded.

Daoju did not reply, did not falter, and did not halt.

Perpetua turned to Godspeed. "Won't you ask her where she's going? Look at the time!"

Daoju was unlocking the door when he spoke. "Baby, where are you going?"

"Out," she said, and glanced over her shoulder at him, her hand on the doorknob.

"Out where?"

"Out of this house, away from you two. God, you make me sick!"

"Daoju!" Perpetua cried out, half rising in her chair. "What did you say?"

Godspeed flapped his hand at his wife. "Calm down, sit down." To his daughter he said, "That's going too far, Daoju. You can't talk to your mother and me that way. Close the door and come back here."

"I'm not coming. I am going."

Godspeed held the arms of his chair and levered himself to his feet. Pointing his finger at Daoju, he raised his voice. "I'm warning you, young lady, come back here now!" Then he coughed, his breath wheezing in his chest.

Daoju threw back her head and laughed as her parents watched in amazement. Then she looked her father in the eye and spat out, "You're not man enough to stop me from leaving this house." The door banged shut behind her.

Perpetua faced Godspeed. His hands were shaking, his lips trembled, he seemed about to fall over. She felt the urge to clap in his face, to tell him that all those years he had spoiled their daughter, treated her like a wife, this is what it amounted to, a door slammed in his face. Yet when she opened her mouth the words wouldn't emerge. She pitied him, quivering in front of her without shame or the pretense of a fighting spirit. Victory is not stomping an opponent that something else had laid low. She rose, walked up to him, and took his arm. At the touch of his skin, warmth flowed into her; compassion quickened her breath. She eased him back into the chair and said, "Easy, my dear, forget what she said. She's just angry at the way things are. She'll come back and apologize, you'll see."

The words barely out of her mouth, Perpetua cocked her head and listened, sure she had heard the gate. There were footsteps approaching. "I told you, she's back already," she said in a triumphant tone, and sat down beside her husband to await Daoju's entry.

The front door burst open and Daoju stagger-ran in, fell in a sprawl. Perpetua screamed, clapped a hand to her mouth, then slid out of the chair and sank to her knees. Six, seven, eight men barged in through the door, bearing automatic rifles. The man in front had a crowbar hooked over his shoulder, and another grasped a machete, its blade glistening red. Godspeed, as he rose from his seat, glared wildly at Daoju, searching for blood.

"You, fat man, down on the ground!" ordered the man with a crowbar on his shoulder.

Godspeed dropped to his hands and knees, crawled quickly across to his daughter, and lay facedown beside her. Perpetua, too, stretched out on her belly and covered her head with her arms. Low sputtering sounds emanated from her, and, now and again, like an expletive, she hissed, *"Jesus!"* One of the men stepped forward and nudged her thigh with his mud-crusted boot. "Get up, prayer warrior. Show us the money."

As Perpetua led them through the house they slapped her eleven times. They ransacked the bedrooms, took her jewelry box, her daughter's gold locket and antique silver charm bracelet, her husband's red coral studs and ivory cuff links and Breitling wristwatch, all the valuables they could find, all the Anabrabas had left. Then they returned to the sitting room and kicked Godspeed, beat him with their fists and gun butts, cut his forehead, sprained his arm, and broke his ring finger as they yanked off his wedding band, but in spite of the punishment, despite the threats, there was no money to be got. When they demanded the keys to his car and he gasped out that he had none, the robbers had enough.

"You want to waste our time?" the crowbar robber yelled. "You live inside this big house and you're a fucking poor man!" He paused, glanced at Daoju sobbing in her father's arms, and a gleam entered his eyes. "But we won't go just like that. We will teach you a lesson." He turned to his men and said, "I go do the girl first," and then unslung the crowbar from his shoulder and tossed it to the floor, where it clattered loudly. "Bring her here. Make una start with the woman."

"Over my dead body."

After he spoke, Godspeed climbed to his feet. His right arm, swollen at the elbow, was cradled in his left hand, with its broken finger hanging by skin. He stared at the line of men, and they glared back—bristling like hyenas circling for the kill—and raised their rifles.

"What did you say?" the crowbar robber barked. He strode forward a few steps, looked Godspeed up and down. Then he said, in a low, mellow voice, at once a tone of warning and reasoning: "If you want to die, repeat what you said."

Someone tittered with excitement. The robbers waited for Godspeed to beg, to plead for his women, to back down. With each second that ticked, the scent of blood grew thicker.

"Daddy, please, it's all right," Daoju whispered, and stretched out her hand to her father, her face a mask of dread. Perpetua, sprawled on her side, did not stir.

"Daddy, please, listen to your daughter," one of the robbers lisped. Then he grabbed his crotch and thrust his hips rapidly back and forth, to raucous laughter.

Godspeed glanced down at his daughter and saw the infant he once saved, and he turned away, his jaw trembling. He stared at the ceiling, bit his swollen underlip, and renewed his pledge. He would not fail. He was ready; only one thing remained. He looked at Perpetua, stared at her bowed head until she sighed weakly and raised her face. *I love you too,* he mouthed. Her eyes widened, moistened, and she brushed the tears away, anxious to hold his gaze. Then she nodded—and was still nodding when the grandfather clock tolled.

A Nairobi Story of Comings and Goings

Let's call her Leo. White, thin, auburn-haired, South African. Clan mother to waifs, yet childless herself, monthly mourning missed chances. Fierce as the Chinese dragon, green and red inked, bug-eyed and fire-spitting, tattooed on her back, under her left shoulder. Rebel, polymath, denim-jacket-and-jeans-wearing Leo, swaggering helter-skelter in her grubby tennis shoes, puffing her reefers with a GI Jane sneer, holding her own with the playground bullies, the boys.

—If you're a white woman in Africa, penises are not your problem. Arse envy is.

That's Leo for you.

ॐ

Leo liked factoids, UN statistics, Wikipedia. The first time we fucked, afterward, she said:

—You are the twenty-five percent.

(Seventy-five percent of men ejaculate two minutes after penetrating.)

ॐ

The setting, Nairobi: the multiracial mix of people, the idiosyncratic weather, the sights, the sounds of that gray-stone city. I traveled to Nairobi for a change of scenery, and to get as far away as possible from my stepmother, who had started befriending my girlfriends in an effort to get me to settle down. With careful management of my savings, I figured I could afford a month of laziness. So I applied for a two-month visa, and flew second-class on the cheapest airline out of MMIA, the crappiest airport in the world. Lagos to Nairobi via Addis Ababa. It was my first trip outside Nigeria, and the more countries I passed through the better, I had thought; also, Addis Ababa was a beautiful city, everyone said, a city ringed by hills and steeped in mist and history. Wisps of mist and distant hilltops were all I saw through the glass walls of BIA's Terminal II, where I remained for six hours—unable to pass immigration because I had no Ethiopian visa, afraid to close my eyes for fear of bag snatchers, with nothing to do but ogle airline hostesses—waiting for my connecting flight, just another Nigerian in a noisy crowd of raffia bag-lugging cheapskates. After that experience in its best airport, at the hand of its national carrier, Ethiopia can keep its history.

JKIA is the second crappiest airport in the world.

ॐ

The engine of Nairobi is fired by cash-crop farming, oiled by tourism, and steered by NGO money. Everywhere you turn in the city you find NGO people, camouflaged by straw hats and safari boots and the skin color of the tourist, white. In the supermarkets (Indian-run), the swanky restaurants (white Kenyan–run), the bus parks, souvenir bazaars, immigration offices (black Kenyan–run), luxurious hotels and safari lodges (British-run), AIDS patients' wards and spoken-word poetry slams (American-funded), and, in small sightseeing groups, in Kibera, the largest zoo in Africa.

ॐ

I had a Facebook friend, a Rwandan living in Nairobi, who met me at the airport and drove me to the apartment in Kilimani rented with money I had wired him. After removing my shoes to relieve my altitude-swollen feet, I walked in tow round the bed-sit shaking my

head at the scuffed floorboards, the threadbare velveteen chairs, the
bathroom tub rimmed by scum the color of lead, the shit-stained
Armitage Shanks, forced to feign approval because the Rwandan
thought we all lived in shanties in Nigeria. He worked for a Belgian
NGO, wore Italian designer shoes, and affected French manner-
isms. Four days after my arrival we quarreled over my intimacy with
Leo, he unfriended me on Facebook, and that was that.

Leo worked for an NGO too, a British concern with regional
offices in many parts of black Africa. Before she was dispatched
to Nairobi for a special project, she worked in the Cape Town
office. The main office in West Africa was sited in Accra, Ghana,
and she had been there, but had visited Nigeria as well, several
times. She liked Nigerians (passionate, assertive people) and she
was proud of her grasp of pidgin. Her dope dealer in Cape Town
was Nigerian.

Leo was not your average NGO person. She was no Mother Teresa,
she did not like Nelson Mandela, she dressed like a Wonderboom
roadie, she disdained Bob Geldof's song and dance, and, unlike her
colleagues—who fucked like goats, within the flock—she took local,
non-NGO lovers. About her job, she said:

—You know how it is, it pays good money, and I've earned it,
I've done my bit, I served the ANC when it was still high treason,
I played my part in the struggle, and now, how do you Nigerians
say it, man must . . . what's the term, it means *eat* . . .

—Man mus' wack.

—Ja, that's it. Man mos wack. No be so, broda?

ॐ

I met Leo the same evening I arrived in Nairobi. Some NGO
people were throwing a party for a colleague who was returning to the mother ship, berthed somewhere in civilization, and
the Rwandan took me along. A place called Sippers on Argwings
Kodhek Road. (As we drove past the road sign I asked about the

source of the name, but the Rwandan had no idea. Sounds Klingon, I said; and his rejoinder: Is that one of the Nigerian tribes?) The restaurant was packed, tables were arranged outside, several parties were going strong, and the noisiest was a mainly white crowd gathered around two pushed-together tables. The Rwandan headed straight for this group, and to a raucous chorus of animal noises, sat at the table. A hush fell as I, too, sat down.

—This is my friend from Nigeria. He arrived today. He's in Nairobi on vacation.

Among people of a certain economic status, the word *vacation* is as potent as *open sesame*. I was good people, a gourmand, a hedonist, a connoisseur of the finer things in life, their expressions seemed to say. The silence lifted, the smiles beamed forth, the drinking glasses tinkled, and soon I found myself plied with questions from all sides.

—What do you think of Robert Mugabe?

—Obama has been a huge disappointment, wouldn't you agree?

—Not to be rude, but why are so many Nigerians engaged in e-mail fraud?

—How about you get away from those wazungu and come sit beside an African sister?

That was Leo, slouched in her seat at one end of the table, her tennis shoe–clad foot propped on the table's edge, a reefer dangling from her lips. From the first she was brazen, meeting my startled gaze with a twinkle in her smile. I moved to her side.

Introductions were dispensed with. She was a fast talker, a nonstop talker, a fish in water with words, instinctively articulate. In twenty minutes I knew enough about her to be intimidated. By this time she had offered me her reefer to finish, and also pressed on me her glass of whiskey (Black Label, she stressed), though she borrowed it now and again to sip from, her eyes holding mine over the rim. She had crazy eyes, crafty eyes, bewitching eyes, benevolent eyes, depending on how the light reflected off them. Most times it reflected crazy.

—Let's get out of here.

Like a crash of thunder, out of the blue—clichés for a clichéd feeling, surprise. Until she said those words I wasn't sure she was flirting with me.

—You're in Nairobi to play, aren't you?

I muttered that I guessed I was, and Leo, with a histrionic flourish to her actions, threw back her head and drained the last of the whiskey, slammed down the glass, swung her foot off the table, then leaned in close, so close that I saw the color of her eyes, gray flecked with green.

—Come on, big boy, she said. It's Friday night. Let me show you Nairobi.

ॐ

Nairobi is a city of cats, abandoned creatures, conceited, territorial, basking on rooftops in the pale sunlight, yowling defiance through the long cold nights, hunting, frolicking, spawning in the grass of private gardens and public parks: once upon a time the roaming grounds of lion prides, lone-ranger leopards, man-eaters, now taken over by cast-off pets.

Nairobi nights. Essence of the city. Distillate of dissipation.

The life force of Nairobi resides in pockets of the Central Business District—River Road, Kirinyaga Road—and on the outskirts in Ngara, in Gikomba market, and extends more or less eastward all the way to Eastlands. Grotty, untamed Nairobi—the ground marshy with discarded ugali meal and rotting strings of sukuma wiki, the air reeking of goat and pork nyama choma and writhing under the snarl of matatu engines and outdoor speakers blasting Swahili talk shows, Sheng hip-hop, English-language commercials.

Nairobi's middle class, tourists, and NGO people steer clear of
this part of town.

⁂

Leo took me to a tented restaurant cum live-band bar on the corner
of Muindi Mbingu Street, a place called Simmers. It was an oasis
of Congolese rumba and modish prostitutes right smack in the
center of the office block-colonized CBD. As we walked in under
the glare of halogen light and curious stares, she bumped me with
her hip, hooked her arm through mine, and said:
—Welcome to Nairobi, drunks and lovers.

⁂

The rib of a young goat roasted to perfection and garnished with
garden-fresh, zingy kachumbari, three glasses of Scotch whiskey,
half of a reefer and a dozen sticks of Embassy Lights, two hours
after arriving at Simmers, and the conversation with Leo began to
flow. I became, I found, more appreciative of her wit, her acumen,
less watchful with her, more confident of the nature of her attention. We talked about me, about my preoccupations, my impres-
sions of Nairobi, and also about our two countries, our abused
continent. Several times I fell silent in midsentence, surprised by
the loudness of my voice. One of such times, while talking about
an ex-lover whose image rose in my breast with the sharpness of
heartburn, Leo said into the silence:
—You're sweet. And that's so fucking sexy.
Sometime after, during a lull in conversation, Leo gazed around,
bobbed her head to the loud, percussive Lingala music, and then
said:
—See that malaya, at the bar, the one wearing the orange kanga
dress? Ja, don't point. Check out her bum.
The girl was built like a wasp, hips for miles and a Barbie waist.
—I'll invite her over.

Leo rose, pulled her denim jacket tighter around her shoulders, and weaved through the crowd of drinking, smoking, sweating dancers, headed for the bar. I watched as she drew up beside the girl, touched her elbow, bussed cheeks in greeting, and began speaking with her. When she turned to point out our table, I looked away.

—Haai.

Leo and the girl stood in front of the table. Leo rocked on her heels, her cheeks flushed with pink, her eyes darting between my face and some point over my head. The girl's face wore a rigid, I-don't-care expression.

—This is Agnes.

—Hi, Agnes, I said.

—Have a seat, Leo said, and pulled up a chair for her. What's your drink?

—Tusker malt, Agnes said. She had sat down across from me, and she looked up over her shoulder as she answered Leo, craning her limber neck, her coral drop earrings swinging.

—One Tusker malt coming up. Anything for you, babes? No? Right-o. Back in a flash.

With Leo gone, Agnes turned her attention to her purse on the table, then to the dancers swirling around us, and finally to me.

—The mzungu says she's your girlfriend.

I nodded yes, surprised.

—She seems older than you.

I shrugged. She was. Seven years older.

—Where did you meet her?

—Right here, Nairobi.

—You don't sound Kenyan.

—I'm Nigerian.

—Ah, Nigeria, Agnes said, a wistful smile parting her bronze-glossed lips. I have a son for a Nigerian. Chinedu, that's his name, my son. He's six.

—And his father? Does he live in Kenya?

—No. He's in Tanzania now. Doing business all the time, like a Kikuyu.

—Where are you from? Your ethnic group, I mean.

—I am Maasai. But my mother is Kikuyu.

Leo returned. She handed the beer to Agnes, then turned her chair around, straddled it, and folded her slim, blue-veined arms across the backrest. Her posture announced she was in control.

—I saw you two talking. How do you like Agnes so far?

—Very much, I said, and smiled at Agnes. She smiled back.

—I thought you would.

Something in Leo's voice drew my gaze. Her face was turned to Agnes.

—He likes your arse. I guess that's all that matters. I hope you're cheap enough.

Agnes raised the beer bottle to her lips, watched Leo as she gulped. When she set down the bottle, it was empty. She picked up her purse and rose.

—Thanks for the beer. I'll be at the bar when you're ready.

୬

The first time we quarreled I thought she would cry she was so angry, so full of feral energy. Afterward, when our breaths had calmed, as we shared a spliff in bed, our skins gummed with sweat, limbs entangled in exhaustion, I told her she fucked as she fought, like a cat.

—No, babes. I'm a dog, a real bitch in fact, she said.

୬

We danced, Leo and I, swinging our hips to frenetic Soukous music—our breaths mingling, groins brushing, hands stiff with awkwardness, mine at least. At three-something Nigerian time (I hadn't reset my watch) Leo settled the bill, and we walked out of Simmers, Leo with a prance, me weaving side to side to keep my world in balance. We approached a parked taxi and Leo bantered with the driver, their voices floating to me as though through a long tunnel. When they were done I pulled the car door open, climbed in after Leo, and my last memory of that night is of the gentle rocking of sea waves.

&

We fucked as the urge came, Leo and I. She was playful, experienced, generous in sex, her pale skin exotic, her soft hair strange; and she had a "natural mystic" that I found irresistible, bags of it stashed around her penthouse, and half-smoked fat ones burning in crystal ashtrays beside the bed, feeding the haze in which we drank whiskey punches, snacked on Pringles and pawpaw, petted Sankara, and fucked again.

&

Sankara was Leo's cat, a gray-striped tom. He was still a kitten when she found him under a hedge in Nairobi, half-dead from starvation, abandoned by his mother. (When Leo was seven, her mother took her one summer day to Clovelly Beach in Cape Town, and while she played in the sand, her mother walked into the sea, never to return.)

&

I woke up to the smell of coffee and scrambled eggs. I was lying facedown on a settee, fully clothed except for my shoes, my cheek wet with drool, my head ringing like a kettledrum. When I got to my feet everything felt strange, the weight of gravity, my putty knees, the gnawing in my belly, the room I was standing in. Then Leo said from behind me:

—Rise and shine, sleepyhead. It's a beautiful morning.

Grinning at me. She stood in a wide doorway that opened onto bright sunlight, a reefer stuck in her mouth and a spatula in her hand. Her long hair was tousled, the wavy, reddish-brown tresses framing her face like a mane. She had on a loose white gown, under which her nipples were mauve circles, and through which sunlight filtered, showing her long pale legs and the shadow of her pubes.

—Morning, Leo, I said. Then I stretched; the pain in my stiff-ened muscles made me groan.

—Come sit on the terrace, the fresh air will do you good. I'm rustling up breakfast.

She turned and went through the doorway, and I followed. It led to a rooftop patio, and her kitchenette was there, built to one side. Leo stood in front of an open fridge, arm stretched out in bless-ing, fingers rummaging in the frost. A cat was sprawled on its side beside the fridge, its head turned to watch me with ginger eyes, its banded tail sweeping slowly across the floor. Leo swung the fridge door shut with a whump.

—Haai Sankara, he's a friend, she said to the cat, and bent down to stroke his pricked ears. She straightened up, turned away, and Sankara eased to his feet, padded to the end of the patio, leapt lightly onto the wall, and dropped from sight.

I stood watching as Leo popped bread slices from the toaster, then sawed an orange in half and squeezed out juice. She brushed back hair strands from her forehead with her wrist, blew out weed smoke from the side of her mouth, and darted glances at me as she worked. Then I moved forward, to the wall of the patio, and looked down at Nairobi, stretched out under me in every direction. Judging by the nearest buildings, identical apartment blocks in a walled compound, Leo's penthouse was eleven stories high.

Leo laid out breakfast on a wrought-iron table on the patio, poured steaming coffee into two cups (she drank nothing but Kenya AA, the best coffee in the world, she told me later), and then called me to eat. As I sat at the table, I asked:

—How did I get up here last night? I have no memory of climbing stairs.

Leo answered, straight-faced:

—I carried you up.

I was the same height as Leo, or maybe slightly shorter, but besides being a man, with bigger bones and a thicker build, I was black and she was white. So I laughed at her joke, and picked up the butter knife.

—I'm serious. I piggybacked you. You were snoring like a tuk-tuk. One hundred and eighty-seven steps to the top. Know what that is? Pure murder.

℘

Her nipples were tender, she felt queer in the mornings from the life growing inside her, she was sure of the signs. Happy days, those days when we both were nervous with hope. We'd gone days without a fight, days of weaving dreams about motherhood and second chances, the childhood we never had. Then her period came. The fights started again.

℘

After breakfast I told Leo I had to go, but she persuaded me to spend the day in her apartment. I didn't take much convincing. She had a Jacuzzi, a comfortable four-poster bed, food and weed and lots to drink, and a Venus de Milo–shaped bottle of euca-lyptus oil with which she planned to massage my tired muscles. The only problem was she also had plans for another night of club-bing, and I didn't have a change of clothes. So she offered to take me shopping.

We drove to the supermarket in her official car, a tinted-glass Land Rover. She parked by the door of the butcher's, right next to the medium-sized supermarket with an Indian nameplate. We got down, she beeped the car locked, and her mobile phone rang. She pulled it out and glanced at the screen.

—I have to answer this, babes. You go on ahead, take anything you want, it's on me.

℘

The last time we fought I had just told her I loved her. She said *actions not words,* and that if I did truly I would give her a baby, I would never leave her that way, not really.

—Love means coming back even when you can't.

Then we quarreled.

I got my things and left.

℘

First thing I noticed when I entered the supermarket was the check-out counter, three cash registers squatted on it, manned by a triad of Indian women, who by their ages could have been daughter, mother, and grandmother. I greeted them as I passed by. The daughter looked up and nodded, the mother turned her face aside, and the grandmother, her watery eyes magnified by spectacle lenses, stared fixedly at me. I picked up a shopping basket and turned into the nearest aisle.

A clutch of shoppers browsed through the supermarket, and the attendants, five that I counted—three women and two men, none of them Indian, all wearing yellow aprons—were busy assist-ing shoppers or stacking shelves or mopping the floor. I had come shopping for undershorts, T-shirts, socks, haberdashery. While searching for these items I found a few other needs: a toothbrush, a can of deodorant spray, a graphic novel of *Othello,* two bars of milk chocolate, one for me and one for Leo. Then I stopped in front of the pastry shelf, checking out the cookies. Overcome by choices, I decided to pass, took two steps, and changed my mind. Whirling around and starting forward, I almost bumped into the youngest of the cashiers, the daughter.

—Are you looking for something? she asked. You've been stand-ing here for a while.

—As a matter of fact I am. I need some T-shirts and boxer shorts.

—Well, you won't find those among the cakes. Please come this way.

She walked to the front of the store and called to a female attendant who was arranging milk cartons in a glass-front refrigerator, asked her to leave that alone and show me the clothes section.

—Assist him with any other thing he wants, she said as I was led away.

The attendant stuck to my side for the rest of my shopping. She watched as I selected three colors of Fruit of the Loom T-shirts, two sets of cotton boxers and an undershirt, some socks, and a pair of gray woollen gloves. I moved across to the pastry section, and she plodded after me, not bothering to turn away when I threw glances at her. My plan was to browse through until Leo arrived, but I felt so uncomfortable that I decided to pay and leave.

I walked to the checkout counter. The mother and daughter were attending to shoppers, but the grandmother was free. I halted in front of her and placed my basket on the counter.

—No, no, no, go that way, she said, shaking her head and pointing toward the other cashiers. So I picked up my basket and went to stand behind the shopper who was being attended to by the mother. While I waited my turn, a straw-haired man with sun-reddened, peeling skin, dressed in a sleeveless T-shirt and faded canvas slip-ons, approached the grandmother and plonked down two packs of Marlboro, a six-pack of Coors Light, and a box of Durex Ribbed.

—Shikamoo, Mrs. Desai. Habari gani?

—Jambo, the grandmother answered with smile. Then she rang up the items and called out the total. While he counted out shillings, she bagged his purchases. You have a good day now, you hear, she said as she handed him the change.

The shopper in front of me picked up her bags and moved off. I stepped forward, set my basket on the counter, and drew out my wallet.

—Remove the items from the basket, the mother said, without

looking at me. Then she beckoned to the next in line, a plump, mixed-race woman with an empty baby carrier strapped to her chest. The woman hurried forward, jostling me aside with her shopping trolley crammed full of baby things, and began unloading them onto the counter. The mother picked up a pack of Pampers from the woman's pile, checked the price tag, and tapped the cash register keys.

—Excuse me, I said. I was here first.

She picked up a box of cereal, ignoring me.

—I'm talking to you, madam, I said in a hoarsened voice. My chest was tight, and I felt like reaching forward to grab the woman's shoulders, to shake the neatness out of her primped hair. If nothing else, that would force her to look at me.

—Don't raise your voice here, she said in a firm, quiet tone, as if speaking to a child. Then she picked up another item, a jar of yogurt.

A lifetime in a country of a hundred and fifty million black people was the worst preparation for what I was faced with. Shame, incredulity, emotions too fresh to label, washed over me. But the inflammable, anger, rose higher fastest. I drew in breath to bellow, but caught myself when a hand fell on my shoulder.

—What's going on, babes?

Sandwiched between the urge to vent my anger and the burden of explaining, I spluttered, swung my face back and forth, glared at Leo and the cashier.

The mother had stopped tallying the items; she stared up at Leo with tight-lipped haughtiness. Then her eyes shifted to my face. Saw me for the first time.

—I'm sorry, there's been a mistake, the grandmother said. She had risen from her seat, and now she hurried forward, grabbed my basket handle. Please come this way, I will attend to you.

—No, Leo said. Her hand gripping my shoulder tightened, and her voice hardened, unsheathed its steel. Let this bitch do it. I saw everything. So what's the problem, his money ain't good enough for you?

—Now, now, the grandmother said, wheedling. No need to be abusive.

—Fuck you too, old woman, Leo said in a high, quivering voice. You bloody coolies fucking disgust me. You do this pussyfooting apartheid shit all the time, everywhere you go you take your shitty caste mentality. You picked the wrong bitch to try it on this time, I can tell you.

Leo was so angry I felt my own anger dissipate. I felt protected, and proud to be so fiercely defended, and, at that moment, watching the rage rise crimson to her thin-boned face, I felt my chest expand with something close to love. But I also felt a shiver of pity for the three generations of women watching dumbstruck from behind the counter.

I faced Leo, placed my hands carefully round her waist, and drew her tensed frame against my chest. Then I spoke in a whisper, lips brushing her ear:

—You're sweet. And that's so fucking sexy. Let's go home.

She sank against me, purring without sound, and her hands crept up my back, rubbing, tugging my shirt. Her arms were stronger than they looked; they squeezed the breath out of me, tightened vicelike until I felt her heartbeats against my chest, matching my wild heart blow for blow.

And then we left.

∽

Because I said I loved her. I did, at that instant, coming in her. But love does not mean marriage, a baby, forever. Love means you make me happy until you don't.

Acknowledgments

Acknowledgment is due to the following publications, where stories from this collection originally appeared, some differently titled or in slightly different form: *AGNI, Black Renaissance Noire, Eclectica, Guernica, Happano-no-Kofu, Internazionale, Kwani?, Kweli Journal,* the *Drum,* and *TQR.*

I'm grateful to the Chinua Achebe Center for African Writers and Artists, the Ebedi International Writers Residency, the Norman Mailer Center and Writers Colony, the Rockefeller Foundation Bellagio Center, Storymoja Publishers, and Farafina Trust for their support.

To many I owe enormous thanks, especially Anwuli Ojogwu for friendship, and Doreen Baingana for reading, never pulling punches, always challenging. Michela Wrong, Binyavanga Wainaina, David Kaiza, Eghosa Imasuen, Jeffery Renard Allen, my editors Fiona McCrae and Parisa Ebrahimi, all the good folks at the Wylie Agency, and not least my family, Barretts and Oruwaris—appreciations.